BREAKING HIM

SHERILEE GRAY

Entangled Publishing, LLC
2614 South Timberline Road
Suite 109
Fort Collins, CO 80525
Visit our website at www.entangledpublishing.com.

Scorched is an imprint of Entangled Publishing, LLC.

Edited by Karen Grove
Cover design by Cover Couture
Cover art from iStock

Manufactured in the United States of America

First Edition September 2016

entangled
scorched

For my friend and CP, Nicola Davidson—I'm glad I don't have to do this without you.

Chapter One

The dry Montana heat was unforgiving today. Dust coated the back of my throat, my sweat-slicked skin prickling from the harsh midday sun. The thunder of hooves drew my attention from unpegging the laundry and over to the field behind the house. Two of my horses galloped along the fence line, kicking up more dust as they passed. I lifted my ponytail from my sticky neck and shielded my eyes to watch.

They slowed, danced around each other, sizing the other up.

Beautiful.

I wiped the sweat from my brow and looked to the sky, searching for rain clouds. We were in the middle of a drought, suffering the highest temperatures we'd had in over ten years. I had animals to feed, a ranch to keep afloat. If the rain didn't come soon, I'd have the bank manager out here again, hounding me. These were the things that should be occupying my mind as I tugged the last towel from the clothesline.

But how could I concentrate on any of that with the low, steady murmur searching me out, coming to me on the light breeze? The way that gravelly yet soothing voice was being used to gentle one of my skittish mares made me tingle all over, until I was forced to squeeze my thighs together.

Folks around town called Elijah Hays a monster. They were intimidated, scared of him. Even said he was dangerous. Not to his face. Never to his face. You'd have to be a stupid son of a bitch to say any of those things to Eli—and crazier than they accused him of being. But I'd never seen him that way. Not once. I trusted him to take care of my ranch just like my father had.

The ranch's main income came from cattle, but with the drought and everyone selling stock to get by, unable to afford the feed, cattle prices had dropped to an all-time low. If we sold now, we'd never recover. We usually survived the dry season by selling off the wild horses we brought in and broke for a nice profit. My dad loved horses, had wanted to eventually expand that side of our business. But this year, with him gone and only Eli here to work them, I didn't know if we'd make it through.

Pushing back the strands of hair that had come loose from my ponytail, I turned to watch him, unable to help myself. How could I see him as the townspeople did when I witnessed him like this each and every day? Eli had a way with horses unlike anyone I'd seen. It fascinated me, watching this huge, at times unnerving, man care for and baby them. The way he could break a horse with kindness—taming, bending them to his will with whispered words and those big, gentle hands—until they seemed desperate to please him.

He stood beside the mare, one hand gripping the wide brush, dragging it over her shiny coat, the other following in its wake while he whispered sweet nothings in her ear. My attention was drawn to his forearms, corded and veined, dusted with dark hair. Pure strength. His hands never left her once. And God, they were beautiful hands—huge and so damn rough. I knew this because when I brought him coffee in the afternoons, his fingers would brush against mine. But what had my nipples hardening against the soft cotton of my dirt-streaked tank top was his unbelievably wide back. It was bulked up with thick slabs of lickable muscle, deeply tanned from hours spent outdoors. My gaze dropped to soft, worn Levi's sitting low on his hips, cupping an ass that was meant to be squeezed, and often.

But if what people said was true, no one had ever squeezed that magnificent ass. No one had seen what he had hidden behind that straining zipper, either…

He swept the brush across the mare's side again and again, biceps—thick as one of my thighs—bunching and rolling, dancing as he worked. I'd never seen the likes of him in my life. The man was beautiful, masculine on a whole new level. And he absolutely fascinated me.

The sound that had been steadily building in my chest slid past my lips before I could stop it. The needy moan loud enough for him to hear. I spun around before he caught me staring, quickly bending to pick up the wash basket at my feet. But it was too late. I'd been caught. The rhythmic cadence of Elijah's deep voice cut off suddenly, followed by the crunch of gravel under his boots as he spun around.

He didn't say anything. He rarely did, not to me—besides the "please and thank yous" he quietly rasped whenever I brought him food or drink. Otherwise he kept to himself. Had done so since he started working here twelve months ago.

I shivered again, that familiar zip of electricity shooting across my shoulders and down my spine. His eyes were on me. He had beautiful eyes, wide and thickly lashed. They were often on me, maybe as much as mine were on him. I liked it. I didn't see Eli as a monster. Because if he had murdered his father when he was just a boy, like everyone said, the man had deserved it. My dad, God rest his soul, had said so many times.

Said Wyatt Hays had been a mean son of a bitch and he was surprised no one had done it before his son took a kitchen knife to him defending his mom.

But the folks here were still wary of him. I'm sure people who visited Deep River thought they'd stepped back in time. The people born in our isolated, backwater town generally lived and died here. And that's the way they liked it. Anyone different from them...scared them. They didn't like the way Elijah rarely spoke, the way he kept himself apart. Though plenty of the women liked the way he looked just fine. I'd seen the lust-filled glances cast his way. Still, they kept their distance, would never dream of approaching him, frightened by his dark past, the gossip that surrounded him. His size and strength were intimidating, not that I'd ever seen him use them against anyone in anger.

No, Elijah preferred his own company, and I didn't blame him. Not when he'd only ever been subjected to the ugliest versions of everyone around him.

When he wasn't busy with the ranch, he was reading, or giving the sand-filled bag he'd suspended in the corner of the barn a beating.

He was a mystery, and I hadn't gotten any closer to him, learned any more about him, in the six months since my father passed away and I took over running the ranch. Because despite the way he watched me, he sent off unmistakable don't-come-any-closer vibes that could be felt fifty yards away.

"Miss Abigail?"

I jolted in surprise, goose bumps popping up all over my skin like an icy breeze had washed over me at the sound of his low voice edged with that delicious growl. Elijah never initiated a conversation. Not when he didn't have to. His voice sounded cautious, gritty, nothing like the tone he used on my horses.

My heart galloped faster as I turned on shaky legs. I

plastered a smile on my face, forcing my eyes to stay above his shoulders. "Oh, hey, Eli," I said, like I hadn't been acutely aware of his quiet, dominating presence the whole time. Eli knew his job better than I did. The only time I sought him out was when I needed him to come to town and help me collect supplies. I usually just wrote what needed doing on a notepad in the barn, and he did it. I squinted against the sun, taking several steps closer, laundry basket resting on my hip. "Mare's looking good."

His brown eyes were locked on mine, making me squirm. He dipped his chin, dark hair that was darker from sweat falling forward across his brow.

Damn, the man had a way of looking at a person, direct, unwavering. Telling you without words that he didn't care what you thought about him, that he didn't care one whit if you believed all the talk about his past or what your opinion was about it, either. I didn't know if that was true or not, or if it was a defense mechanism he'd built to protect himself, but it was unnerving as hell.

I retreated a step. "Right, well, I'll leave you to it. I have to…ah, go get ready." He didn't say anything, just kept his steady gaze locked on mine, and as usual my mouth ran away with me, trying to fill the inevitable silences when we were alone. "I've got a date, you know, with Kyle, so I better…"

Something flickered behind his eyes, something that had the skin crinkling at the corners—not from a smile, no, he never did that—he looked tense, strained. That square, scruff-covered jaw was tight. His Adam's apple slid up and down the front of his thick neck before his expression smoothed out, once again impassive. My eyes dipped, like someone else had control over their movement. His sudden discomfort made my thigh muscles clench, wanting to move me closer, to brush his hair back and search his gaze until I knew what caused that unease.

Then my brain registered what my eyes were looking at, and I sucked in a breath at the sight of his bare chest. Something about his size…his bulk… The brown hair that dusted his pecs, bisecting his deeply ridged abs, all the way down to the waistband of his jeans, made me lose my breath every damn time.

Those tight abs tightened further, and my eyes darted up. Color darkened his broad cheekbones, but that was the only sign that he'd caught me ogling him. His rugged features remained arranged in their usual inscrutable position.

The strong and sudden urge to force him to react, to tempt him past his control — to climb that massive, ripped body, wrap my thighs around his hips, and hang on while he bucked into me like an ornery bull, snarling and grunting until we were both spent — was near overwhelming.

Then I noticed the way his powerful fists clenched and unclenched at his sides. It wasn't threatening. He was uncomfortable. Guilt swirled in my belly. He may watch me sometimes, but he'd never given any indication that he wanted more. He was happy with the horses, with his own company. I hated that I'd made him uneasy. He'd had enough of that his whole life, being stared at like a sideshow freak. I refused to be lumped in with the gossiping townsfolk whispering behind his back, speculating, judging. Eli wasn't the kind of man you toyed with, and I'd been reminded six months ago, as my dad was lowered into the ground, that close ties, relationships… love, only ever caused pain.

"Well, it's getting late…"

He motioned to the overflowing basket in my arms. "Let me."

At those two words, just an innocent statement, my heart jumped forward, smacking against my ribs, my quickening pulse relocating itself between my thighs. "I've got it. Thanks, though." I stumbled back another step. Like I had two left feet. "You have a good evening, Eli." Then turning away, I hustled my ass inside.

And somehow I knew his intense stare followed me the whole way.

. . .

"Girl, I'm sick of your damn teasing." Kyle dragged his sweaty hand higher under my skirt. "You finally gonna give me what's under here, or what?"

There was a slight slur to his voice, a slur I hadn't noticed when we left the bar. "How much did you have to drink? You said you only had a couple beers."

He shrugged. "A few shots as well." He grinned in a way I knew he thought was charming, but with a gut full of beer and whiskey, he just looked like a big, dumb idiot.

I'd known Kyle since high school. Back then he'd been a chauvinistic, irresponsible asshole; it seemed nothing had changed. When he'd asked me out a month ago, I'd decided to give him the benefit of the doubt, hoping he'd matured. The fact that he was good-looking, built, and had all his teeth may have played a part in my decision to give him a shot. Not to mention an eight-month-long dry spell and an itch that needed one hell of a good scratch. But nothing was going to happen here tonight. Not now, not ever.

I shoved the passenger door open and slammed it shut behind me. His door wrenched open as well, and he rounded the car fast. Grabbing my arm, he hauled me back and pinned me to the car before I'd barely taken two steps.

"Where d'you think you're going?" He pressed into me, the liquor on his breath invading my nostrils. "Time you paid up, honey. I've done the time, taken you out, bought you a burger, drinks, all that shit. Time to give it up."

I shoved at his shoulders. "You've lost your goddamn

mind, Kyle Harris." I tried to wriggle free, but he wasn't having any of it. "Back the hell up, get in your car, and get out of here."

Grinding his hard dick against my leg, he grunted and nipped my earlobe, yanking my shirt down over my shoulder. "Cock-teasing whore. What the fu—"

Kyle was on me one minute, then being pulled away the next. My jaw went slack as Elijah, fingers wrapped around the back of Kyle's neck, dragged him like a sack of potatoes to the driver's side and slammed him face-first against it. Kyle flailed and cursed while he was being manhandled. The door was yanked open, and Eli shoved him in like his own personal rag doll, then slammed it shut behind him.

The expression on Kyle's face as he blinked up at the big man through the window was priceless. He looked shit-scared when he realized who he was staring at. The car started a second later, then it was gone the next, leaving a cloud of dust in his wake.

My gaze shot to Eli. I don't know how it was possible, but the man looked even bigger, muscles flexing, jaw tight, nostrils flaring with each angry breath. "Elijah?" I took a step toward him, and he jerked back suddenly, shock covering his face, before he turned and stormed toward the barn. The bang of the door after him was loud, echoing through the quiet night.

I had two options: I could go inside like a coward and pretend what just happened hadn't, or I could go after him, thank him for coming to my rescue, and attempt to erase some of that worry I'd seen in his dark eyes.

Wiping my sweaty hands on my skirt, I headed toward the barn. It was still hot out, but there was a breeze, and the light floaty fabric of my skirt whispered around my thighs. Anticipation ignited low in my belly as I neared, then the deep, repetitive thump of those solid fists connecting with the punching bag in the corner of the barn reached my ears.

I'd heard the same sound often as he beat the crap out of that bag, but this time was different. He was hitting harder, faster, working off his anger and frustration. Maybe I should be afraid. Maybe going in there now was a damn stupid idea, but I couldn't make my feet stop, couldn't make them turn me around. Pressing a hand to the barn door, I pushed it open and stepped inside.

The familiar scent of hay and motor oil hit me first. Every light was on, throwing a golden wash into the corners. A tractor took up one side of the barn. Tools and other equipment were scattered on the workbench that ran the length of the wall. On the other side was a rough wooden staircase that led to Eli's rooms, and in the corner, beating the hell out of that bag, was the man himself.

I stood there motionless, unable to take a step closer, yet I couldn't turn and walk out, either. As if he sensed me, he stopped abruptly and spun around. His wild stare crashed with mine, and I sucked in a breath. Every ripped muscle, vein, and tendon bulged. He'd obviously tugged off his shirt when he'd walked in, because now his chest was bare and glistened with sweat. He was breathing heavily, fists still clenched tightly.

"Miss Abigail?" he said through panted breaths.

Despite that wild stare and the way his body throbbed with aggression, when he spoke, none of it came through. His cheeks were dark from exertion, mouth slightly parted as each heavy breath pumped from his lungs, struggling to maintain control, but still he hadn't directed any of that anger at me.

I managed to unglue my feet and started toward him. He seemed to brace himself as I moved closer, hands on hips, back and shoulders stiff. When I stopped in front of him, instead of his direct stare, he aimed his eyes at the ground. "Eli?" He didn't move, didn't speak. Reaching out, I touched his arm. "Elijah?"

He jolted, muscles tightening under my fingers. God, I felt

tiny standing this close to him. He finally answered, voice low, "Ma'am."

My nipples tightened painfully. He didn't pull away. "I just…I wanted to thank you for what you did back there."

His head was still down, not allowing me to see those dark eyes. Without thought, I reached up, threading my fingers in his hair, and tipped his head back. My only thought had been to get those eyes on me again. I *needed* them on me.

My belly dipped and swirled at the rough sound that tore from his throat. I was about to pull away, to apologize, but he tilted his head, pressing more firmly against my palm, moving the tiniest bit closer. Finally, he raised his chin, thick lashes lifting, and I had them. My body zapped, sparked, breath escaping in a rush, heat curling and growing like a wildfire was spreading over my skin.

"You like my hands on you?" I whispered before I could think better of it.

His breathing had grown ragged, a softness, a vulnerability in his eyes that made me want to give him everything I didn't think he'd allow himself to ask for. His gaze darted to my bare shoulder, where Kyle had yanked my shirt down, and his wide chest expanded with his sharp inhalation. He didn't like the reminder of what happened, of Kyle touching me that way.

"Do *you* want to touch me, Eli?" I could barely believe the words that just came out of my mouth, but I didn't want to take them back, I wanted those massive hands on me, had wanted them on me for the longest time.

The tip of his tongue darted out, sliding across his bottom lip, then his head dipped, just a fraction.

"You do, don't you?"

He stared down at me, his large frame, thick with muscle, towering over me, looking like he could pick up that tractor beside us and fling it halfway across the field, which made the almost innocent curiosity, the restrained excitement he was currently aiming my way all the more surprising.

"Yes," he rasped, cheeks darkening further.

He made no move to touch me, though, kept his arms at his sides, fingers curled in loose fists, bracing for I didn't know what. I reached down, taking one of his hands in mine, lifting it slowly. The skin was as rough as I remembered and hot, so damn hot. He smelled of clean sweat, the outdoors, the soap he used. The combination was incredibly sexy. I uncurled his fingers and rested his hand just above my heart. My top was low cut, so we were skin to skin, and my body went up in flames from that simple touch.

I watched him, gauging his reaction. His eyes were locked on his fingers. His hands were scarred with cracks and gouges, dark and stained, as clean as they ever got. The contrast against my lighter, smooth, unblemished skin was startling—exciting.

"Is this what you want?" I asked softly.

He dipped his head again, fingers flexing slightly, stare intent, scorching.

"More?"

"Yes…please."

Oh God, the way he said it, deep, rough… I jammed my legs together, the throb between my thighs making me reckless, making me do things, say things I might not usually. But here in the barn, so quiet and still, it was just us and this moment. I couldn't stop even if I wanted to.

Wrapping my fingers around his thick wrist, the coarse hairs tickling my skin, I lowered his hand slowly, until his palm grazed the swell of my breast. "You ever touched a woman here, Eli?"

He shifted his weight from one foot to the other, jaw tightening, then shook his head.

I could barely believe it. No, he didn't talk much, kept to himself, but he was smart, gorgeous, and a harder worker I'd never met. "Why not?"

He didn't answer, just kept his eyes locked with mine. An answer wasn't necessary. I knew why—the same reason everyone in this town kept their distance. Fear. I moved his hand lower, struggling to breathe when the rough skin of his palm dragged over my hard, aching nipple. He swallowed audibly and made another one of those hungry, low sounds.

"Your skin's so hot," I whispered, curling my fingers around his, encouraging him to squeeze me. He flexed them, but he didn't let up this time, no, he pressed in, tightening around me in a way that had me soaking my panties. "Feels good?"

"Yes, ma'am." When he said those words, there was a spark of something thrilling in his eyes. His nostrils flared. "Better than good."

Dear God, it was. What the hell was I doing?

Chapter Two

Eli's throat worked as he gripped my breast tighter. His hand looked giant covering me, engulfing me completely. His breath was choppy, getting harsher by the second. Then he pressed his palm deeper, a soft huff bursting past his firm lips as he moved his hand in a tight circle that had my legs close to giving out. When he squeezed again, pleasure shot straight to my core, wringing a whimper from me. His gaze slid to mine and he stilled, then slowly, he ran the rough tip of one finger across the top of my breast, lifting goose bumps instantly, before starting its descent toward the center.

He took his time, like he was relishing the feel of me, the discovery. His eyes were laser focused, nostrils flaring with each labored breath. That torturous finger continued until it bumped the top of my nipple. My breath jammed in my throat when he began to circle it slowly, methodically. I whimpered again, and he shuddered as he dragged his fingers lower, cupping me again, lifting me, then started sliding his thumb back and forth over the tight, hard point, watching my response.

I was going to come. I was going to come from just that alone…

A car door slammed, jarring me, followed by the sound of boots taking the steps to my house. Someone knocked. "Abi?" a gruff voice called.

I stilled. *No. Please God, no.* I wanted to scream in frustration, to pretend I hadn't heard it. "It's Garrett," I whispered, voice breathy, barely recognizable. My father's oldest friend often dropped by unannounced.

Elijah yanked his hand away like I'd slapped it.

"Eli…"

"Sorry," he gritted out. "I shouldn't have…I should never…" He backed up a step.

"Elijah…wait…"

He shook his head, took another step away, then turned and strode out the side door of the barn and into the night.

Garrett had returned to his truck, calling my name. I wanted to go after Eli, but I knew if I didn't go and talk to Garrett he'd freak out.

The barn door creaked open before I could head out. "Here you are, girl." His bushy brows raised high, relief covering his face. "I was out in my yard and saw Kyle tear past looking madder than hell." He pulled off his cap. "Came to check you're okay."

I'd told Cassie, his wife, about the date tonight. They both worried over me, more so since Dad passed. "I'm fine." I led him to the house, reassuring him as we went, but once he finally left I had barely any recollection of what I'd said to him—not when all I'd been able to think about was Eli's hands on me.

• • •

The next morning, nerves dive-bombed my belly as I headed

outdoors. Every third Friday of the month, Eli drove into town with me to pick up supplies. It was already hot as hell; not a breath of wind so much as ruffled my blond hair, which I'd left loose for a change. I'd gotten my light hair and petite frame from my mother. My wide green eyes and delicate facial features—my dad used to call me pixie—came from my father's side of the family. And I was glad of it. Glad I didn't have to see her every time I looked in the mirror.

I always made an effort on our shopping trips—a little makeup, one of my dresses. If I didn't wear them when the opportunity arose, I'd never get the chance. Well, that's the reason I'd always told myself. This morning, though, I'd taken extra care, pulling on my favorite yellow sundress and brown boots that were worn in just right, with one thought on my mind—getting Eli to react to me the way he had last night.

My belly fluttered, pulse quickening. What would he do when he saw me? Had I scared him off? I didn't know what had come over me, or why I wasn't just trying to forget it, pretend it never happened. For all I knew, with the way he'd run off last night, he'd either try to avoid me forever or leave the ranch.

But I didn't really think so, not after the way he'd reacted.

I blew out a breath. God, I had no damn idea what he'd do, how he was feeling, and it was making me crazy.

I'd tossed and turned all night, aching and hot, unable to think about anything but the way he'd stared at me when I'd asked him if he'd ever touched another woman the way he'd touched me. That glint of excitement in his eyes. All of it had swirled through my mind till the early hours of the morning, until it drove me out of bed, desperate to see him again.

Because I wanted him. I wanted Elijah Hays in a way I didn't understand, a way that had me behaving as recklessly as I had last night. In a way that kind of scared me. I wanted to be the one to show him how good it could be. To be the one to make that big, muscular body quake, to make him moan until his voice was grittier and rougher than it already was.

I rounded the barn, my steps faltering when I finally saw him. He was leaning against the side of the truck. Soft, worn Levi's hugged those long legs, straining over his solid thighs. He wore a dark blue T-shirt that clung to his wide shoulders, stretching around his massive biceps. I couldn't see his face with his head dipped, the brim of his ball cap concealing all but his square, scruff-covered jaw. But he'd stilled, in that unnatural way he did when I was around him, like he was holding his breath...or tracking me like a predator about to pounce.

As I approached, he lifted his chin, the peak of his hat coming up, but not enough for me to see his eyes.

"Ready to head out?" I asked, trying to inject some lightness in my voice but failing miserably. I didn't feel light, I felt weighted down, restless. He wouldn't want me to bring up what happened, but he also hadn't run, so I was counting that as a win.

He dipped his chin again and, shoulders tight, rounded the truck like he always did, opening the door for me. After I got in, he climbed behind the wheel, fired up the engine, and we headed out. The drive was a quiet one, which wasn't any different from the other trips we took to town, but this time the space between us seemed charged. Eli's unique scent, a heady mix of dark spice and outdoors, combined with the truck's leather seats, surrounded me, had my heart racing, made it impossible to think of anything but him.

And the way he white-knuckled the wheel, forearms bulging and corded, jaw locked tight, I knew he felt it, too, the tension, the undercurrent of something magnetic firing between us.

Once we hit town, we made our usual rounds, picked up the supplies we needed, and three hours later the truck was loaded up and we were ready to head back.

He'd barely said two words to me the whole time. That wasn't unusual, either, but after last night it frustrated me. I wanted more from him. "I'm kinda hungry. You wanna get lunch?"

"Coopers?" His response was immediate, almost eager, but said with a gentleness that drew my belly tight.

Eli liked watching me eat. I knew this because the times when we went to Coopers, he did just that, after he'd made short work of his own lunch. I'd keep my head down, focus on my food, pretending I wasn't aware of his hot gaze on me, the satisfaction in the tilt of his lips when I finished everything on my plate. I didn't really understand it, but I liked the way it made me feel.

The smell of fresh coffee and fried bacon hit us as soon as we walked into the cozy diner, making my mouth water. We took our usual seats, the far corner in front of the window. Elijah's back to the wall, mine to the door.

He rested his hands on the red Formica table, and I couldn't help but admire them. I really did love his hands—wide palms, fingers thick and long. It always amazed me how he could toss a bale of hay like it weighed nothing, swing an ax like nobody's business, and hit that bag of sand in the barn like he wanted to tear it apart—but how gentle he always was when he tended the horses.

And now I knew how they felt on me…

Our breakfast arrived, and in his usual style he tucked in, demolishing it like it was his last meal. Then he pushed his plate away and sat back. His fingers curled around his coffee mug as he took a sip, his eyes sliding from the view out the window to me. A bolt of lightning shot through me. My nipples hardened instantly, and I locked my knees together. I'd been trying to ignore the persistent throb between my legs since I'd laid eyes on him this morning, but squeezing my thighs together put delicious pressure on my swelling clit and a moan slipped out before I could bite it back.

I ducked my head and shoved a forkful of bacon and scrambled eggs in my mouth to cover it, but he'd heard. He was doing that still-as-a-statue thing he always did. He liked it when I took pleasure in my food, as much as he liked to watch, but he had no way of knowing the real reason I was moaning, why every inch of my skin was oversensitive, too damn tight for my body. I was turned the hell on, so much so that my appetite vanished completely. I pushed my plate away as well. "We should get going."

I went to stand, butt in the air, when those long fingers curled around my wrist, setting off sparks of pleasure all the way up my arm. I looked up at him, and he shook his head. "Finish." Heat climbed his cheeks, but his eyes stayed locked on mine.

"I'm not really…"

"Please," he added gruffly. "You've barely eaten."

I blinked at him, a million questions firing through my head at once. I lowered to my seat and dragged my plate back to me, desperately trying to conceal my shock at the pleased look that crossed his face, gently curving his lips. For some reason this was important to him. Why? I wasn't comfortable asking, but I'd choke down a whole damn pig's worth of bacon to see that look on his face again. To experience this unexplained tingle of pleasure I got from pleasing him, just one more time.

I didn't pretend I didn't know he was watching when I took my next bite. I kept my eyes on him. Under the brim of his cap, I could see the glitter of his gaze, unwavering, locked on my mouth as I ate everything on my plate. When I licked my lips, his parted slightly. A small tell, but one just the same. Knowing he was getting off on watching me made me squirm in my seat.

When I pushed my plate away it was nearly scraped clean. "Ready?"

He stood, then came around and held my chair as I got up. We headed back to the truck.

Thirty minutes into the drive, I risked a glance his way. I'd been studiously looking out the passenger window, trying to get myself under control. Sitting in that diner while he watched me the entire time had my underwear soaked through and my heart trying to jump out of my chest. His chin was low, sun glinting off his scruff. My fingers itched to reach out and touch him, to experience the texture against my fingertips—other places.

That strong, square jaw tilted, the peak of his cap slanting toward me slightly, and his eyes slid from my knees up between my slightly parted thighs. He licked his lips then turned his attention back to the road. The urge to jam my legs together again was almost too hard to resist, but he didn't know I'd seen him, and the thought that he'd been sneaking looks the whole time we'd been driving made me even hotter. I looked down at his lap and had to swallow a moan. His cock was hard against the front of his jeans.

Oh God, I couldn't take much more. I wanted that big cock inside me, badly, so much so that I'd be going straight to my room when we got home and fucking myself silly with my vibrator, thinking of Eli powering into me the whole time. Okay, that thought wasn't helping me cool down, not one damn bit.

I shouldn't, but I found myself reaching down, taking the fabric of my dress between my fingers at each hip and sliding it a little higher up my thighs. When I glanced at him, his head was tilted my way again. He'd watched me do it. His chest was pumping now with his labored breaths, knuckles white, gripping the wheel, and his cock—I bit my lip—Jesus, it was huge, straining his jeans like it was trying to bust through.

I was contemplating sliding across the seat, releasing that enormous dick, and sucking it dry when Eli wrenched the wheel to the right. He'd nearly driven by the long dirt road that led to the ranch. He didn't look at me after that, just continued to grip the steering wheel like his life depended on it. When we reached the house, he drove up beside the barn and slammed on the brakes. Not waiting for the cloud of dust to settle, he shoved his door open, got out, and after coming around and opening mine, still without looking at me, he moved to the back of the truck. The tailgate dropped open a moment later, with more force than necessary, and I spun in my seat, watching him haul a bag of feed out of the back, his solid biceps bulging as he flung it over one massive shoulder. He strode toward the barn, long legs eating up the short distance.

I shivered.

The urge to go after him was almost too hard to ignore, but I hurt, that's how turned on I was. So instead, I climbed out of the truck, ignoring my own supplies, rushed inside, and went straight to my room. Yanking my bedside drawer open, I grabbed my vibrator, shoved down my underwear, tore off my dress, and collapsed on the bed, my floral quilt cool against my overheated skin. Spreading my thighs, I imagined Eli on top of me, his mouth on me, those hands everywhere, rough and demanding. I was breathing faster, anticipation clawing at me. Need so fierce my thighs shook. Trailing a hand down my belly, I spread my labia and circled my clit. "Oh God."

I was so damn empty. Pressing the blunt end of my vibrator against my opening, I slid it deep, thrusting it in and out, over and over. It was cool and hard and not what I wanted, but it would have to do. I worked myself for a while, trying to get there, but it wasn't Eli, and both my mind and body knew it...

A sound like a groan hit my ears, and my eyes flew open — colliding with Elijah's.

He stood at my partially opened bedroom door. My shopping bags from the back of his truck on the floor at his feet. One hand gripped the doorframe; the other squeezed the massive bulge at the front of his jeans.

Neither of us moved. His labored breaths were loud, so loud I was surprised I hadn't heard them sooner. I should be embarrassed, horrified, but I was too far gone to stop now. Shit, having him standing there, eyes on me while I fucked myself, did something to me, had me on the verge of coming instantly. He wanted to watch.

Wanted me to show him.

He wasn't backing away, and I didn't want him to go, so I slowly spread wider, giving him a better view. His eyes dropped to where I was still working my slippery, swollen clit, and I took advantage, showing him what I liked, what I wanted from him, and worked the vibrator deeper, sliding it in and out slow and steady, tormenting us both.

He made a sound that was half moan, half broken sob, then squeezed his cock harder. His other hand peeled off the doorframe and slapped against the partially open door, hard. It flew open, banging against the wall with force, and he stumbled over the threshold, into my room. He didn't approach the bed, though; he moved to the side, back colliding with the wall, like he needed it to hold himself up, then growled, "More." He licked his lips. "Show me. Please."

Oh dear God. His face was dark, hands shaking, and all the while he crudely massaged his dick through his jeans. He was the hottest thing I'd ever seen. I had no choice. I wanted to give him anything he asked for. So I gave him more. Spreading as wide as I could, I fucked myself harder, faster, my clit sliding under my furiously moving fingers the whole time. A keening whimper burst from my throat—close, so close. I twisted and moaned but never took my eyes off his, the intent, hungry way they watched me, the way his lips parted, tongue sliding out, licking his suckable lips.

I reached up and squeezed one of my tits, tugging, pinching the nipple, and heat shot down my spine, burning through my core, and I blew up. I cried his name, arching against the mattress, screaming as I came so damn hard, light was dancing in front of my eyes.

Eli growled, the animalistic sound bursting through my orgasmic haze, and I forced my eyes open. His were wild, glittering, then he grunted and took a step toward me. We were both panting, gazes locked. I opened my mouth—to say what, I didn't know—but before I could, he stopped suddenly. Torment distorted his ruggedly handsome features, sharpening his cheekbones, hardening his jaw, and a sound exploded past his lips, a sound that lifted the hair at the back of my neck, a cry filled with pain. Then he spun around and stormed from the room. I lay there stunned. I had no idea what he was thinking, but I knew I had to go after him.

Sliding off the bed, I dragged my dress over my head and raced on shaky legs out the door. The yard was empty, no sign of him, so I ran to the barn. The interior was dim, silent; there was no pounding on his punching bag this time. He wasn't down here. I looked at the stairs that led to his rooms. I'd never gone up there, not since he'd moved in. The steps were sturdy, rough against my bare feet, not making a sound as I cautiously took them. His door was closed, so I knocked softly. No reply came, but I knew he was in there. Turning the handle, I pushed the door open, and my breath caught in my lungs.

Eli stood, back to a tall bookshelf, face red, eyes screwed shut, jeans undone, and cock in his hand. He was stroking the long length with sharp, brutal tugs.

That alone was hot enough, but something about seeing the magnificent man in front of me, his tall, built body against a shelf full of well-read books—it was the sexiest thing I'd ever seen.

Oh dear God, he was magnificent.

Without thinking about it, without saying a word, my only thought to have that beautiful cock in my mouth, I crossed the room and dropped to my knees in front of him. "Let me," I rasped.

His eyes flew open, and he tried to back up. "Jesus, I'm sorry...I didn't mean..."

I reached up, wrapped my fingers around his, and his body jerked like I'd given him an electric shock. "Let me," I repeated.

"Miss Abigail," he gritted out. "You shouldn't..."

I climbed to my feet, gripped the bottom of his shirt, and holding his gaze, lifted it slowly, giving him the chance to tell me to stop, that this wasn't what he wanted. He didn't. He stared back, and the way he looked at me made my pulse race.

I dragged it up over his powerful body. He had to lean forward so I could pull it over his head and fling it aside. "I want to make you feel good." Then I leaned in, wrapped my lips around one of his flat brown nipples, and sucked and licked it. He moaned and began to shake as I dipped lower, tracing the ridges of his abs. I groaned when I finally got a taste of his warm, salty skin. Damn, so much better than I'd ever dreamed—and I'd dreamed a lot.

His cock was as impressive as I suspected it would be. I knew I couldn't suck all of him down, but I could make it damn good. Dropping to my knees again, I wrapped my fingers around the engorged base and sucked the fat purple head into my mouth.

He shouted, hands going to my shoulders, and shoved me back. "Jesus Christ... What are you...?"

His cock pulsed in my hand when I squeezed it, cutting off his words, and his deep groan made my belly quiver. Pre-come leaked from the tip, coating my fingers, and I slid my fist up and back. "Do you hurt, Eli?"

Every one of his muscles bunched and tightened, and a gasp burst free. "You don't have to do that." He moaned, hips rolling. "Christ…so good…"

For some reason his words tore at my heart. I darted my tongue out, tasting him. "Do you want me to? You taste amazing." I leaned in, nuzzled the dark hair at the base of his cock, drawing in his musky scent, and looked up at him. "I want to."

"Why?" Vulnerability mixed with something dark and breathtaking clouded his eyes.

I slid my free hand up and down one of his rock-solid thighs and locked eyes with him. "Because you want me to. Because *I* desperately want to."

"You like it…the way I taste?" He was blushing again, uncertainty in his voice, and it equally turned me on and destroyed me at the same time.

"Yes." I slid my tongue over the head of his cock again. "Hell yes." His expression was one I'd never seen before on Eli, pain and excitement, maybe a little fear. It thrilled me. "Did you like watching me get myself off?"

"Yes," he growled.

"I'd get the same pleasure from watching you." The next words formed in my head and I almost didn't say them, but somehow I knew Elijah needed them. "I just want to please you, Eli. Have you…have you thought about it, us together? Me, on my knees in front of you like this? I have."

He groaned, more pre-come spilling from his dick. "Yes." He let out a ragged groan. "Yes, goddammit."

I nearly whimpered. My thighs shook, slick with my arousal, throbbing again like I hadn't made myself come just a short time ago. "Just tell me you want this, tell me you need it as much as I want to give it to you, and I will, Eli. I'll make you feel so good."

His abs tightened, hips jerking forward like he had no control over them. Then he looked down at me, conflicting emotions moving through his dark eyes. But trumping them all was heat, so much heat, it scorched me in the best way. When he finally spoke, his words sounded torn from his throat, tight and raspy with need.

A shudder quaked through his body. "Please…suck it. Suck my cock."

Chapter Three

"Do you have any idea how many times I've imagined doing this to you?" I gripped his length more firmly, wrapping both hands around the wide base, the skin smooth and hot beneath my fingers, against my palm. "You're big, Eli. Bigger than any man I've seen."

He moaned and shook his head. "Don't." He pressed his hands against the shelf behind him. "Don't tell me about anyone else, I can't…just don't."

Oh God.

I kissed the fat, swollen tip. "It's just you and me." I darted my tongue out, tasting him once more. "No one else." I started to jack that impressive cock with both hands, then leaned in and sucked the head deep into my mouth, taking him as far as I could. He shouted, both hands hitting the bookshelf on either side of him hard enough to make the windows rattle. Releasing him with one hand, I dragged my nails up the side of his massive thigh, then reached around and gripped one muscular ass cheek and squeezed. Pulling back, I put my tongue to good use, licking him from root to tip, lapping the ridge, getting off on his harsh breaths echoing around the room, his seductive scent getting stronger, the way his eyes were locked on what I was doing to him. I kept at it until his abs looked cut from stone and his thigh muscles were jumping.

He bucked, a desperate sound ripping from his throat. "Darlin'… Darlin', please. I can't take much more."

Christ, the sound of his voice, the way he'd just called me *darlin'*, I was close to coming again and I hadn't even touched my swollen clit.

Tilting my head back, I looked up at him as I reached for one of his hands, prying it off the shelf and placing it at the back of my head. I sucked him deep, and his fingers immediately burrowed into my hair, holding on. I sucked harder, and his low groan seemed to shake the ground beneath me.

"Shit," he barked and tried to pull back. "Gonna come…"

I stayed where I was, then he was coming, shaking and growling, hips jerking as he pumped hot and hard down my throat. I stayed where I was until he was finished, then I took my time licking him clean. When I was done, I rose to my feet and did what I'd been dying to do for the longest time. I reached up and cupped the side of his face, dragging my thumb across his stubbled jaw, feeling the texture against my skin. "You're magnificent, Eli Hays." Then, going up on my toes, pulling him down to meet me, I placed a gentle kiss to the corner of his mouth and stepped back.

His breath rushed in and out of his lungs like he'd just run full speed from one end of the ranch to the other. His eyes dropped to my chest, down to the apex of my thighs, and he took a step closer. More than anything, I wanted to go to him, let him do to me whatever was going through his head right then, but I knew if I did, I would never leave this room. Not good, not when I had Garrett's wife, Cassie, popping over for a beer and a catch-up. If she caught us together…well, I didn't know how she'd react. How could I explain it to her, when I didn't know what this was myself?

But that wasn't the only reason I was saying no to anything more right then.

I planted my hand on his abs, shivering at the way those bulky muscles tightened. "I wanted to do that for you. I don't expect anything in return. Things got heated fast. Think about it, whether you wanna go any further with this." I took a step back, and he swayed toward me. My eyes dipped to his already hardening cock. *Sweet Jesus.* "You want more, you know where I am. But if you don't?" I offered him a small smile. "No hard feelings. I'll leave you to your own company and we'll carry on like before, like this never happened."

I hated that idea. A lot. And even as I said the words I didn't know if I believed what I was saying. But I also didn't want to push him into anything.

I took him in, one last time, all heaving, rippling muscle, expression fierce, jaw tight, eyes bright. Then I walked out, shutting the door behind me.

• • •

Sweat trickled down between my shoulder blades, dirt smearing my arms, as I pulled weeds from around my struggling tomato plants. I'd neglected a lot of things after Dad died; it was hard taking on full responsibility of running the ranch. I'd been doing most of the work before he passed on, but we'd been a good team—we picked up each other's slack. It'd been just the two of us for a long time, and I missed him like crazy.

I didn't know why I was so melancholy. I'd woken up feeling low, and that dark cloud had hovered over my head all day. Lifting a hand to shield the sun, I looked out to the field where Elijah was working with the mare again. He had a halter in his hand, letting her scent it, while he continued to touch her face. Getting her used to the sensation, the smell.

The horse's ear pricked up. I couldn't see Eli's face, but I knew he was talking to her, comforting her, encouraging her, praising her as he slid a hand into his pocket for a treat—rewarding her for being a good girl. That's what he'd be murmuring in her ear. "Good girl. That's my girl." His deep voice low, gentle, but with that ever-present growl that lifted the hair at the back of my neck.

There was something in him, something hungry and wild, something I didn't know if even he was aware of. He'd obviously closed himself off from everything and everyone, from his own needs and feelings. Not surprising with the way people treated him. But I knew it was there, lurking just below the surface. A part of him he'd locked down tight, constantly fought against. I craved that part of him. I wanted to be the one to set it free.

I wanted to break through, *break him*—so I could put him back together piece by piece and make him whole again.

Then I wanted him to turn all that newly unleashed hunger on me, have those scarred, rough hands on my skin, demanding, taking whatever they wanted. I wanted him to make me scream his name until I forgot my own.

I wanted him to gentle me, praise and encourage me as he bent me to his will.

A shiver slid through me.

What the hell was wrong with me?

A gust of wind came out of nowhere, whipping around me, and a *crack* rang out as a bolt of lightning rent the sky. I shivered again, but this time for another reason. I hated storms. Had since I was a little girl. Though I'd welcome this one, welcome the fears that came with it, if it would bring blessed rain.

I looked back to the field, and Eli was heading toward the barn, the mare left to graze. Troubled by my thoughts of him, the way they'd affected me, confused me — aroused me — I realized I wasn't ready to face him again just yet. Not when I could still taste him on my tongue, when I could still feel the way he'd trembled under my hands, could hear the lust-filled noises he'd made when he'd come ringing in my ears.

Spinning around, I raced toward the house. Darting up the porch stairs, I slammed the door after me, leaning against it, breathing hard, right as a low, building roll of thunder reached its peak. It was so damn close the windows rattled. My arms flew up to cover my head, and I shrieked.

It was just a goddamn storm, not an omen, or a sign something bad would happen. Logically I knew this, but no matter how hard I tried not to let it get to me, every time one blew through I reverted to a scared kid, waiting for my world to implode. I could still hear my father's voice, competing with the thunderstorm raging outside, lightning flashing, flickering bright through my bedroom window, as he told me my mother had gone away and wasn't coming back. That she'd decided to leave her family and start fresh somewhere else without us. And I could still see the doctor's somber expression, the way he'd shaken his head, eyes sad as he'd walked out of my father's room, thunder rumbling overhead, drowning out the blood roaring through my ears, as he'd told me it was too late, my dad was gone.

Goose bumps prickled my skin. Climbing into my dad's old armchair in the living room, I pulled up my knees, wrapped my arms around myself, and squeezed my eyes shut. I don't know how long I sat like that, trying desperately to block out the sounds of the storm, trying to ignore the way my belly twisted and curled.

Someone knocked heavily on the door.

"Shit." I jumped, the urgent sound yanking me back to the present. Dread instantly unfurled in my chest as I climbed out of the chair and headed to the door. All sorts of scenarios swam through my head, none of them good. The knock came again, this time louder. Gripping the handle, I pulled it open. Lightning split the rainless sky in two, lighting up Elijah's face. His jaw was hard, eyes boring into me, big body seeming to heave with every breath he took.

He pulled his cap off his head. "I came to check on you," he rumbled, giving the thunder a run for its money.

I stared up at him. How did he know? How could he?

His brows lowered. "You always run inside first sign of a storm," he said, like he could read my mind.

It'd been a while since I'd heard him string so many words together. Talking made him uncomfortable for some reason. That he'd come to me, had done something that was hard for him, to make sure I was okay? It hit me like a raging bull. And I just…reacted. I couldn't explain or control it. Before I could think better of it, I'd taken the two steps separating us and literally leaped into his arms, burying my face against his neck, breathing in his comforting scent. He caught me effortlessly, a soft grunt puffing past his lips. He stood stiff for a second, from shock or confusion I didn't know which, then his heavy arms tightened around me, holding me there.

He murmured something against my hair and stepped inside, closing the door behind him. I should have been embarrassed, humiliated by the way I was acting, but right then, I needed someone, needed *him*. I needed the distraction, anything to get me out of my own head, to distance myself from the pain, the memories.

He walked farther into the house. The hand on my ass flexed, the other was on my shoulder, his forearm locked across my back. He squeezed me even closer, then sat on the couch. With him sitting, I ended up straddling his thighs. He was extremely hard, and I bit my cheek to stifle a needy moan. He planted his hands on my hips and scooted me back a little, and when I glanced up at him, his cheekbones had deepened in color. His face remained impassive, though, concern clearly etched there, eyes darker than I'd ever seen them.

Suddenly I *was* embarrassed of the way I'd acted. Showing weakness like that wasn't me. I never showed my hand, never gave people ammunition to hurt me. And even though I knew Eli wasn't like that, I planted my hands on his chest to climb off him, mumbling my apology. His hands were still on my hips and his fingers dug in, holding me where I was.

I glanced up at him, and he shook his head. Then without a word, he pulled me in, tucking my head under his chin. His fingers curled around my nape, while the other slid down my back to my ass, and he effortlessly dragged me closer, so I was perched on his hard cock, his powerful frame wrapped around me. I sat there stunned. His warmth surrounded me, his smell an intoxicating mix of hay, leather, and clean sweat. We stayed like that for a while, neither one moving. Then finally his fingers twitched and slowly, ever so slowly, he started to rub my back. The movement was cautious, unsure, his heart hammering under my cheek. Mine picked up as well, my breath growing choppy as the need between my thighs grew. The heavy swell behind his zipper got bigger, harder, and I had no control over the way my hips did a little circle, my body reaching for more of his.

My nipples were hard and aching, and the fear had subsided to a low hum at the base of my skull. The need to banish it completely, to have Eli be the one to chase it away, was becoming impossible to resist. He confused me and turned me on like no one and nothing else ever had. The mix of innocence, his size and strength, and that undercurrent of danger and iron control had my head spinning, made me swollen and wet with the need to be fucked hard. The need to have the impressive cock that I was currently grinding against thrusting in and out of me deep and hard.

My hand shaking, I reached back and grabbed his, sliding

it to my front. The pulse on the inside of his wrist as I turned it and pressed it against my aching breast was pounding thick and fast. I whimpered from the contact. "Please. Please make me forget, Eli." I barely recognized my own voice, so filled with unrestrained desperation.

He shuddered, his entire body convulsing under me, then I was off his lap and planted on the couch beside him. At first I thought he was pushing me away, but then his eyes lowered to the front of my jeans and his trembling hands followed, grasping the button, popping it, then sliding down the zipper.

Oh God, I was on fire, burning the hell up.

Gripping the denim on either side of my hips, he slowly dragged my jeans down my legs and threw them aside. His nostrils flared when he stared down at my pink underwear, growling when I parted my thighs shamelessly. His hand dropped to my thigh, so wide it spanned the width, then slid higher until it reached the point my thigh ended and the aching heart of me began.

He swiped his thumb over my opening, through the soaked fabric of my panties, and I bucked and arched. His eyes darted to my face, then down again as he snagged the fabric at my hip and tore right through. I gasped in surprise, and his eyes immediately shot back to mine.

He paled. "Sorry…"

I shook my head. "No. I liked it. Don't apologize."

"You did?" His gruff question had my heart squeezing. It also had liquid heat sliding down the crack of my ass, had me throbbing so hard and deep inside it was like my sex had its own heartbeat.

I released a shaky breath. "Can't you feel how wet I am, Eli? That's for you. You make me so hot I ache."

His wild stare dropped between my thighs again, and he tore through the other side of my underwear before I could drag in another breath. Then he growled and pressed his thumb between my swollen lips, sliding up to my clit, then down to tease my slick entrance. I collapsed against the couch cushions, arching so hard my back hurt. It didn't matter, though; the only thing I was aware of was the ache between my thighs, the burning need to come, to have one of those thick fingers shove deep inside me. I whimpered again, begging, "Please. Please, Elijah."

A tormented sound burst from him, his rough palm covering me, applying much-needed pressure. My tightly shut eyes drifted open as I tried to grind down on his palm.

He leaned over me, eyes dark with lust and wide with concern, with a helplessness that tore me apart. "Tell me," he rasped. "Tell me what to do to make it better, darlin.'"

Chapter Four

His deep, smoky voice slid through me, adding to the out-of-control feeling coiled tight in my belly. He was killing me — the way he moved, his harsh breathing, it all just sent me higher. I was nothing but sweet, delicious agony, and every twitch, every subtle movement of that wide palm resting against my sensitive flesh, made it hurt so much more. Made it so much better.

I'd never experienced hunger like this, or this extreme intensity. What Elijah had me feeling caused a pleasure-pain that was almost too much to take. I panted, trying to catch my breath. He was still staring down at me, eyes dark, intent, concerned. He ground his palm against me again and I cried out, lifting my hips as best I could so I could grind back. My skin was fevered, slick, tight, my whole body throbbing, aching.

"Tell me if I'm hurting you," he demanded roughly.

I furiously shook my head and reached down, wrapping my fingers around his wrist, holding him there, scared he'd go away. I'd die if he stopped. "I'm close, Eli," I managed to gasp out, then stared him in the eyes. "Push your finger inside me…you know…you know what I need…" A wave of indescribable heat pounded through me, cutting off my words. I squeezed my eyes shut, undulating against the cushions. No longer human. A thing, a creature. Sex and need, nothing else, nothing more. The only thoughts in my head now were of Eli, of how badly I needed him to get me off.

He tugged the bottom of my shirt, and my eyes shot open. He gripped the material in his fingers and dragged it up, pulling it off completely with one hand. His gaze dropped to my chest, and without a word, he slid those fingers under the front of my bra and tore it off like he had my panties. My breasts bounced free and my hard nipples pebbled further, tightened almost unbearably when the air hit them—when Eli's heated stare landed on them.

Then I couldn't think anymore, could only concentrate on breathing and not hyperventilating when he spread me open with his fingers and pushed one inside. At the same time his other hand engulfed one of my breasts, squeezing and tugging.

"*Oh God*. That feels so good." My eyes drifted closed, and I was washed away on a wave of pleasure. I rolled my hips against his hand, encouraging him to go deeper, move faster—to fuck me with his fingers until I screamed.

"Open your eyes," he gritted.

They felt weighted down, but I forced them open. His voice held a rough command that I found impossible to ignore. His dark chocolate stare trapped mine, and I held my breath, biting my lip as he slid out of me, then pushed back in, this time adding a second finger. He stretched me with his fingers, shoving deeper, moving faster.

"Shit," I said on a gasp. "Don't stop, please don't stop." My eyes were still so heavy, but the way he watched me demanded I not look away, that all my focus stay on him. It was intimate, making my belly squirm, and I was powerless to do anything but give him what he was asking from me.

His gaze turned more intense, more focused, then he slid

his thumb over my clit, the broad callused pad pressing into the oversensitive bundle of nerves. I bucked and moaned, near out of my damn mind.

"Talk to me, Abigail. Tell me if it feels good." His voice was gruff, urgent, with an undercurrent of concern.

"Yes!" I dug my nails into his skin, close to begging.

His breath came out on a shaky exhale, then he leaned over me, using some of his weight to hold me down, and finger-fucked me deep and fast.

He didn't take his eyes off me once, watching my reactions to his touch, to what he was doing to me. He slid his thumb over my clit again, and I shuddered, a sob bursting past my lips. Something flashed through his gaze then, something I couldn't name, couldn't process, before he dipped his head and sucked one of my hard, aching nipples into his mouth, surrounding it in wet heat, and tugged with his lips.

I screamed, my orgasm slamming into me so hard it felt like an out-of-body experience. My inner muscles clamped down on his fingers repeatedly, and I moaned and writhed and whimpered through every spasm, lost to sensation.

When I finally came back to myself, Elijah's harsh breaths filled my ears. He was moving, quick, jerky. I opened my eyes, and another moan slid past my lips. He was hovering over me, fist planted in the cushion by my head, shirt off, jeans undone—cock in hand.

The vein in his neck pulsed heavy and hard, strain lining his rugged features. He gasped when our eyes met, widening like he'd been hit by a dose of reality. Like he'd been knocked out of the haze of lust we'd both been submerged in.

"I'm sorry..." He made a sound, deep and raw. "But I have to..."

I shook my head. "Don't...don't ever apologize for taking what you need. Not from me." Then I did something I'd never done before, never cared to, but now the idea had me burning up all over again. Reaching down, I grabbed his hips. "Come here." I scooted down as he shuffled up. His cock was unbearably hard, thick and veined, the tip slick. I wanted it inside me more than anything, but I didn't know if Eli was ready for that. So instead I gripped his dick, slicking pre-come down his ridged length, lubing him up as best as I could, and guided him to my chest. His cock was heavy and hot, resting between my tits, and I grabbed the aching mounds and squeezed them tight around his iron-hard length.

He hissed. "What are you…?" I squeezed harder. "Ah… shit." His hips snapped forward.

"That's it, Eli…move," I encouraged.

His heavy thighs were on either side of me, and I stared up over his tight washboard abs, defined pecs, and to that strong jaw. His mouth was held in a grim line—then he groaned, the sound trailing off before he thrust again. His bottom lip slid between his teeth, and he bit down.

He was the most beautiful thing I'd ever seen.

His lids lowered then, and he stared down at me, down at his cock as it slid between my breasts. His broad cheekbones were flushed. His eyes filled with the same mindless lust he'd made me feel a short time ago. He didn't look away as his thrusts got more erratic, as he grunted and moaned, chest pumping with each heavy breath.

The man was exquisite.

Then he growled, his hands coming down over mine, squeezing my tits around his cock tighter. "Abigail."

The way he said my name set off tingles across my scalp, then his mouth dropped open and a guttural, belly-zapping sound exploded past his lips.

Hot come splashed my neck, my chin, slicking the way as he continued to pump his hips, milking every last drop. He cursed and moaned through it, not slowing until his cock began to soften.

He stayed above me for several seconds, eyes closed, drawing in big lungfuls of oxygen through his nose, trying to catch his breath.

When his eyes finally opened they were a little wild, unreadable, and butterflies started fluttering inside my belly. He lifted his hands from mine and pulled back, tilting his hips away. He eased off the couch, down to the floor beside me, so he was on his knees. I couldn't read his expression, but as his gaze trailed over me, the almost fierce intensity there turned to something else, something that looked a lot like awe. My mouth went dry.

He lowered his hand to my ankle, starting a slow, torturous ascent, his touch featherlight, rasping against my skin. Despite my overheated condition, goose bumps prickled my flesh as he continued higher. Over my thigh, my hip, my stomach, then finally up between my breasts. He slid his hand from my chest to my neck, fingers lightly circling it. He held there for several seconds, thumb sliding across my chin, then down, back to my chest. He started rubbing his come over my breasts, down farther to my belly. He almost seemed in a trance, and for the longest time, I lay there while he ran his hands over my body, not moving, afraid if I did, I'd destroy whatever was happening.

His eyes lifted to mine and held. "Beautiful," he rasped. "So small, delicate."

My heart stuttered to a stop, then exploded into action, beating like crazy. I didn't know what to say. I was the experienced one here, and I had nothing. Not. A. Thing. All I could do was watch him watch me, those powerful hands I'd admired for so long moving across my skin like they were worshipping me—taking ownership of me.

I liked the way it felt. Too much.

Then he leaned down and placed a soft, reverent kiss to my forehead. "Thank you," he murmured.

When he lifted his head, my hands moved like they had a mind of their own, sliding along his whiskered jaw, and I pulled him down. He came, didn't try to pull back, and I pressed my lips to his before I could question my actions. We'd never kissed; it seemed weird considering all we had done. The intimacy we'd shared. And I wanted to kiss him, badly.

But when our lips met, he froze, his massive body turning to stone. I softened mine more, brushing them over his, trying to coax a response from him. Reaching around, I threaded my fingers in the hair at his nape, my other hand sliding down over his shoulder, the now-trembling muscle of his monster biceps. My stomach sank. Oh God, he wasn't responding. I was about to pull back, but before I did, I darted my tongue out, selfishly getting the taste of him I craved. That's when he made a sound between a gasp and a groan and leaned in, pressing his mouth more firmly to mine, and finally returned my kiss.

His lips were cautious at first, testing, ghosting over mine. I felt the change in him when it happened. When he went from testing to exploring. The way he pushed back, the way his breathing quickened, huffing in and out of his nose.

Then his mouth opened over mine and his tongue made a tentative dip inside, and oh dear God, it was *good*. I clung to him tighter, and he growled into my mouth, lowering more of his weight on me, catching me up in his massive arms, and deepened the kiss. He kissed me until my head spun, tongue sliding against mine in a way that left me breathless, and I was hot for him all over again.

Finally, he lifted his head, and if someone had asked me how I was feeling at that moment, I would have struggled to find the words. It was bright and dark at the same time. Light and heavy all at once. And I wanted more of it, as much as he'd give me.

I forced an easy smile when he looked down at me, when that was far from what I was feeling. "You're a good kisser,

Eli Hays." My voice shook. "Good" was an understatement. Especially since I was guessing that was his first real kiss. Something else I couldn't get my head around.

His cheeks darkened again in that way I liked so much, but as usual he didn't hide or show he was embarrassed by my words. He didn't say anything, either, or move, he just watched me, weighing my expression like he always did.

Doubt unfurled in my belly. "You're okay, with what… with what we did here?"

Something wicked flickered in his now-glittering eyes. It was sexy as hell. "Yes, ma'am."

The air around us pulsed, shifted. With that one look, Eli had turned the tables on me, letting me know I hadn't led him; he'd taken what he wanted. Like he could see right inside me, like he knew what I hid in the deepest recesses of my heart. I couldn't hold his stare any longer. It was too intense. I looked away. "Are you hungry? I was going to make some dinner."

He dipped his chin and stood. I missed his hands on me instantly. After tucking himself in his jeans, he strode to the bathroom. I was on my feet, pulling on my jeans, commando, since he'd torn my panties, when he walked back in. I could go and get underwear from my room, but I was kind of afraid he'd leave if I left him alone for even a minute. I didn't want him to leave, not yet. He stopped in front of me, halting me when I bent to pick up my shirt. Then slowly, carefully, like I was made of the finest bone china, he dragged a warm, damp cloth over my throat, down over my breasts and belly, cleaning him off me.

Elijah Hays was a man of few words, but his actions somehow did his talking for him. His tender ministrations felt right, perfect, and I edged closer, unable to help myself as he took care of me.

When he was done, he reached down, grabbed my shirt, and finished dressing me. He liked that, too, a lot. I could tell by the look on his face. It was the same expression he got when he watched me eat. A deep satisfaction that made me warm all over.

When he stepped back, I had to stop myself from swaying toward him. I plastered a smile on my face, hoping like hell I hid the way his actions affected me. "I'll go make dinner."

· · ·

I sipped my coffee and glanced out the window. Eli was working with the mare in the training pen. She was dancing away from the halter in his hand. He dropped it to his side and moved in closer. Running his hand along her nose, he lifted it again. She didn't dance away this time...and he slipped it on...

"You know Kyle's been flapping his gums around town?" Cassie said across from me at the kitchen table.

I hadn't meant to be so obvious. I sipped my coffee to hide my reaction to her words and turned to her. "What's that jackass been saying?"

"That Elijah attacked him, unprovoked." Her eyebrow hiked up.

"That slimy little toad. Eli didn't attack him, he sent him packing when Kyle wouldn't take no for an answer. He was protecting me." I snorted. "And Kyle nearly crapped his own pants. That's what has him so pissed. The man looked ready to faint when he saw who'd shoved him in his car."

Cassie made a *hmmm* sound. "I know your dad had a soft spot for the boy, but he's gone now. You don't need to keep him here anymore if he makes you uncomfortable. There's plenty of people that could do his job."

I stared at my friend, surprised by what she'd just said, unease unfurling inside me. "Why would Eli make me uncomfortable?" Okay, he had a time or two, but not in the way Cassie meant. He had me squirming and aching for him, but never scared, never that. "He's a good man, Cass."

She shook her head. "People in town say…"

"Since when do you pay attention to what the gossips say? If what they say he did is true, it happened when he was just a boy. He's a grown man now. From then to now, he's done nothing to deserve the hate and fear he gets from them. They have nothing better to do than make up stories, spouting their poison as fact. Those people know nothing about him, not really. Kyle is the one at fault here, and you know it. And to be honest, I don't know what would've happened if Eli hadn't stepped in." I got to my feet and dumped the rest of my coffee in the sink. "Tell your gossips that."

I turned to Cassie, and she blinked up at me from her seat at my table, then she stood and placed her own cup in the sink. "Well, then. I'm glad he was here to look out for you." She rested her hand on my shoulder and gave it a gentle squeeze. "You have a soft heart, girl. Just like your dad, you give everyone the benefit of the doubt. But, honey, I want you to be careful now that you're here on your own with him. Don't let that handsome face blind you. Something isn't right with that man…the way he doesn't talk, it just isn't…natural."

"Now hang on…"

"His father was a cruel bastard, it's true. No one was sad the day he was put in the ground, but that boy lived in that environment, and for all we know killed the man. Wyatt used to beat him, starve him…"

"What?" I stumbled back a step. *Oh God.* I thought I might actually throw up.

"When he was at school with my boys, the other kids were scared of him. He wouldn't play with anyone, would sit so still and quiet, like a little statue, like no one would notice him if he didn't move…"

"You knew this?" Elijah had moved on to middle school by the time I started elementary and had left high school before I began.

"A lot of folks knew."

"And no one did anything to help him? You all knew his father was abusing him and everyone just sat back and did nothing?" Red rage exploded through me. "You should be ashamed of yourselves…"

"Abigail."

Her voice was sharp, a tone she'd never used on me before, but I didn't care. I was furious. "How dare all of you pass judgment on him when you all let a little boy fend for himself, when you left him living with a monster and did nothing to help him." I was breathing heavily, on the verge of tears, and Cassie was looking at me like I'd lost my mind. She also had the decency to look guilty.

"I regret that I didn't step in, but you have to understand, it isn't done around here. We keep out of other folks' business."

I barked out a humorless laugh. Oh, I knew how it worked around here, the way the people in this town were. "That's horseshit and you know it. This town has more than its fair share of gossips and busybodies. They live to stick their noses in other people's business."

Cassie's expression went from guilt to hurt, but right then I couldn't muster any sympathy for one of my father's oldest friends, for my friend.

"I'm not telling you these things to upset you," she said. "I'm telling you so you know what that boy lived through. He's been…changed, because of it." She put her hand on my arm. "How could he not be after that? You need to be careful around Elijah Hays."

The *bang* of the front door closing cut off my answer before I'd opened my mouth. I raced to the window, cursing when I saw Eli striding away from the house toward the barn.

He'd heard what Cassie said.

He'd heard us talking about him.

Chapter Five

Cassie left, looking pale and kind of freaked out, stuttering her apology. I wasn't interested in hearing it, and as soon as she was heading down the driveway, I rushed to the barn after Eli.

I shoved the door open and stepped inside. It was dimly lit, but I didn't need to see him to know where he was. He was at that punching bag again, beating the ever-loving shit out of it, his grunts as his fists connected breaking the silence.

I walked toward him, not afraid, only concerned, wanting to make it right. To tell him I didn't believe what Cassie said about his state of mind. He might be changed after what he'd been through, anyone would be, but I had nothing to fear, not from him. He'd never hurt me.

He knew I was there—Eli was always aware of his surroundings—but he didn't stop this time, didn't even look at me. His bulging biceps danced as he plowed his fists into the worn leather. I moved in close and reached out, touching his back. He jerked away from me like I'd struck him. "Eli, please stop."

He finally quit whaling on the sandbag and dropped his hands, but he didn't turn to face me. The muscles in his wide back twitched, expanding with every panted breath.

I closed the space between us, moving in behind him, and reached up, resting my hands on his shoulder blades, breathing in his scent—clean sweat and leather. He stilled, like he often did, like I now knew he'd been doing since he was a little boy. Did he wish I couldn't see him, that I'd go away? The idea was a pitchfork through the chest.

Biting my lip, I slid my hands up to his shoulders and leaned in, kissing the center of his bare back, his skin fevered and slick. "I'm sorry," I whispered. "I'm so sorry." I didn't know exactly what I was apologizing for. That I'd been talking about him, that he'd heard what Cassie said, or that the whole town knew what he'd suffered and hadn't lifted a finger to help him. They were small insignificant words, but they were all I had right then, all I could force past my dry, tight throat.

A tremor traveled through him, but he stayed where he was, broad back to me. He was in pain, and I hated that I'd been a part of the cause. It tore me up, and all I could think about was easing his hurt. I moved to his side, my breasts grazing his bulging biceps as I came around to his front. His jaw was tight, eyes closed, locking me out, keeping me at a distance. I hated it, loathed it.

Leaning in, I kissed his chest. His body went tight, every muscle hardening. I continued to whisper my apologies between kisses, tasting the salty, clean sweat on his chest, his ribs, his ridged abs as I dropped to my knees. Fingers trembling, I reached for the front of his jeans. He jolted but kept his eyes closed when I undid the button and eased down the zipper, when I slid my hand inside and took his quickly hardening cock in my hand, pumping the length of him several times.

His nostrils flared, but he kept his jaw clamped shut.

Releasing him, I worked the denim at his hips lower. I

wanted to make this better, but I had no idea how to do that. My gut told me this was what he needed from me. I just hoped I was right.

The metallic scent of blood reached my nose, and I noticed his raw, bleeding knuckles. Taking one of his hands, I pressed my lips to his damaged skin, kissing it tenderly, and that's when his eyes opened and he stared down at me. My own stung at what I saw. There was no anger, not even a little bit. No, there was only shame. He was ashamed of his past, and I could see he hated that I knew.

I leaned in and kissed the head of his painfully hard cock, sliding my hands up and down his heavy thighs and hips. "You have nothing to be ashamed of," I rasped past my dry throat, fighting the tears threatening to escape. His muscles bunched tighter, more pain sliding through his gaze. It killed me, but I was determined to give him what he needed and stayed where I was, on my knees with his eyes locked on me.

We stared at each other for the longest time, my knees starting to smart, pulse racing like crazy, but I didn't move. I waited. Eli needed to take back some of the control he'd lost as a scared kid; he craved it but continued to fight against it. That was what I saw in him, that dark, gritty thing he refused to let free, the part of him I was more than willing to surrender to. Shit, I was desperate for it.

I had no idea what was happening between us, but right then it was like I was gasping for air, like I'd been deprived of oxygen. I needed it to survive, this thing between us—this thing only Elijah could give me.

And deep down I knew he felt it, too.

Slowly, something shifted in his eyes, the pain transforming into hunger. A hunger so fierce, I had to squeeze my knees together when my core began pulsing deep. My lips parted on an indrawn breath as zaps of pleasure fired low in my belly, the excitement building low and hot, making it hard to draw breath.

I watched the fingers on his right hand twitch a second before he raised it, shaking slightly as he slid my hair over my shoulder, then carefully, he gathered it up and wrapped it around his damaged fist.

He spread his legs a little more, bracing his solid body, then gently applied pressure. The strands pulled at my scalp in a delicious way, causing goose bumps to rise across my skin and my nipples to harden to the point of pain. A whimper crawled up my throat, slipping past my lips, when he directed my mouth to the fat head of his cock.

"Open," he rasped, a tortured note to his voice that made me want to do anything for this man, give him anything he wanted.

That one word, said that way, had me damn near vibrating with need. Dizzy with how much I wanted his cock in my mouth, how badly I'd wanted this from him, how much I wanted to give it to him, I did as I was told. I shuffled forward, and then that beautiful dick was sliding past my lips, into my mouth.

His grip tightened in my hair, and I relaxed my jaw. The first thrust came, and his cock went deep, bumping the back of my throat. I forced my muscles to relax more, and on the next thrust he went deeper. I nearly came, even as my eyes watered, even as I dragged much-needed oxygen in through my nose. His grunts filled my ears, his musky scent surrounding me. I dug my nails into his hips, holding him there, afraid he'd stop, afraid he'd pull away.

His grunts got rougher, more intense, then he tilted my head back, and all that dark, dirty heat was on me, eyes blazing, searching mine. I reached down and took his balls in hand, massaging their heavy weight. They drew up tight a second before he growled, and his cock began to throb against my tongue. Come filled my mouth, and I worked my throat, trying to swallow the load. Some slid down my chin, and his eyes tracked it, groaning as he continued to thrust until he was completely spent.

When he was done, his fingers loosened in my hair and he carefully slid from my mouth. I licked my swollen lips, and he grabbed his discarded shirt, using it to clean me up. Then he lifted me effortlessly, my thighs hugging his hips, and he held me tight, his heavy exhales ruffling my hair.

"I was rough with you," he muttered against my temple. "I should never have done that…"

I leaned back so I could see his face and slid my fingers up the sides of his throat, cupping his stubbled cheeks. "It's what we both needed. And Eli," I whispered, "I loved every second of it."

His arms flexed around me, and I dipped my head, kissing his firm lips, letting him get a taste of himself, of the control he'd taken, that I'd been happy to relinquish. His tongue slid against mine, his growling moan working through me in a way that made me want to crawl inside him and never leave. He took several steps, stopping when my ass was on the workbench.

He rested his forehead against mine, our panted breaths mingling. "Are you slick between your legs, Abigail?"

I started to tremble. "Yes."

"Will you let me touch you there again?" His fingers flexed against my ass. "I can't stop thinking about it, how you felt there, darlin', wrapped around my fingers. It's been making me crazy ever since you let me do that to you."

If he didn't, I thought I might break down and cry. "Touch me."

He groaned and tugged at the button of my shorts, then dragged the zipper open, kissing me softly as he slid his hand down the front of my panties, pressing against my slick heat. "Oh, Jesus."

His finger skimmed along my soaked slit, then pressed, pushing inside. I cried out, trying to get closer to him.

"You feel so good. So soft and warm and goddamn perfect." He licked his lips. "Darlin', you're all over my hand." I was gripping his biceps, and the muscles twitched. "I can smell you. Christ, I think I'm losing my mind, Abigail. Making you feel good, it's all I want to do. I never want to stop."

Then he pushed in and slid out. His eyes on me the whole time, watching me, groaning with me when he added a second finger.

My hand slid over his heavy shoulder, up the side of his thick neck, and I fisted his hair. "*Oh God*. Please, Eli. Please…" My hips moved with his thrusting fingers. "I'm nearly there." A sob burst past my lips. "Please…"

His thumb pressed down on my clit and I blew up instantly.

He pressed his fingers deep and held them there, mouth latching onto mine, rough words of encouragement rasped against my lips. "I can feel it, darlin'. You're clutching me so tight, holding me inside. I'd stay there forever if I could, if you'd let me. I'd spend forever making you come like this, listening to your cries. So good, sweetheart. So perfect."

I'd never heard Elijah speak like that, never imagined I ever would. He was as lost to the moment as I was, and it was glorious. We stayed like that for a long time. Elijah only sliding his fingers from my body when I'd finished gripping them. Then he did up my shorts, kissed the top of my head, and carefully lowered me to my feet.

I clung to him, not ready to let him go. We hadn't talked about what happened, what he'd overheard, and despite what we'd just done, what he'd said in the heat of the moment, I was afraid he might change his mind about us, that he might put an end to it…

The crunch of tires on the drive outside had him stilling.

"Garrett," he murmured. "Cassie must have sent him to

check that you're okay." Frustration and resignation lined his features. He released me, his reluctance obvious. "You best go ease his mind."

Of course it would be Garrett. Cassie would have sent him here as soon as she got home, afraid Eli would do something crazy after he heard what she said. My anger flared all over again. I wanted to ignore the man outside; I wanted to stay in here with Elijah, spend all day pleasing him, taking away that pain in his eyes, but I knew if I didn't go out there and show Garrett I was fine, he'd have a lynch mob down here to string Eli up before I knew it.

I lifted on my toes and pulled him down, giving him one last kiss, then I left him and went to reassure an old friend that the gentlest, most kindhearted man I knew hadn't hurt me.

. . .

I pulled the truck to a stop down the road from the bank, turned off the engine, and sat back. The street was fairly quiet, only half a dozen cars parked along this stretch, thank goodness. I wasn't in the mood for idle chitchat. A heavy weight had settled on my chest and wasn't budging. Dad would never have let this happen. As long as we'd lived here, he'd never had Connor Jacobson, the manager of Deep River Bank, visit our ranch, making threats about late mortgage payments. He would hate this. Not just because I could lose the ranch, but also because Connor and my dad had bad blood between them. I didn't know what had caused it, but I knew it went back a long way, and it ran deep. Now it seemed to have extended to me. Connor would love nothing more than to take my ranch from me. I got the impression he wouldn't be happy until he watched the rear end of my truck heading out of town for good.

I climbed out, squinting against the bright sun,

straightened my skirt, and hiked my bag over my shoulder. This meeting was going to be as painful as it got. I already knew before I walked in that he'd more than likely turn me down, but I had to try. I couldn't give up. When the rain came, things would sort themselves out. They always did. I couldn't be the only rancher in Deep River suffering the same low cattle prices, expensive feed. I needed a small extension, just to get us through the next few months.

I shoved the door open and walked into the bank. Cool air blasted me from above. The air-conditioner working overtime, like it always was. That didn't surprise me. Connor Jacobson always looked shiny and flushed, even in the middle of winter. His ever-present pocket square at the ready to mop up the sweat gathering on his upper lip and brow.

Suppressing a shudder, I took a seat on one of the chairs outside his office. The entire room was gray, depressing like a cloudy day, gray carpet, walls, furniture. It definitely didn't help improve my mood.

I hadn't told Eli where I was going this afternoon. In fact, I hadn't talked to him. Not since I'd followed him to the barn yesterday after he'd overheard Cassie and me talking. I'd watched him from my window when he'd finished working on the tractor in the late afternoon. He'd saddled up his horse, his sleeping bag tied to it, then glanced at the house, his expression unreadable, before he'd mounted and ridden out. He did that sometimes, went out onto the ranch and slept rough.

It probably meant nothing—he'd been doing it since he started working for us a year ago—but that didn't stop my chest from squeezing seeing him do it this time. I got it. After what happened, maybe he needed time, space. Things had gotten intense; not just with him overhearing Cassie and me but also between us. It didn't mean I hated it any less that he kept it all bottled up inside. I was also terrified that he'd decide to end this thing we'd started. So I'd waited until I knew he was out working this morning and rushed to the truck. If he did feel that way, I wasn't ready to hear it.

I'd seen him in my rearview mirror, watching as I tore off down the driveway.

It was cowardly. But I wasn't sure I could deal with the possibility of him rejecting me and a meeting with the bank manager, a bank manager who hated my guts, all in one day.

"Ms. Smith."

Connor Jacobson's distinctive deep voice skittered over me, dragging me from my thoughts. I forced a smile and stood. "Mr. Jacobson."

He didn't smile back. He looked me over in a way that made me uncomfortable, setting the little alarm off in my head. The two times he'd been out to pay me a visit, throwing his threats around, I'd noticed the way he scrutinized me, the way he'd take in my grubby shorts and tank and frown. The disapproving look that would pass over his surly features. But today it was different.

"This way."

He waited for me to follow, then closed the door behind us. His shoes made a squeaking noise when he walked around his huge desk and sat down. Wriggling his computer mouse, he clicked around a bit. "Let me take a look at your file."

Like he didn't already know what was in it. Jerk.

"Your payment's late again," he murmured. "This won't do, Ms. Smith. Not at all."

I squeezed the strap of my bag clutched tight in my fingers. "I just need a little longer, Connor…"

His head shot up, and he scowled.

"Ah…Mr. Jacobson."

"You're continually late with your payments. Since your father passed away, you seem to be getting further and further behind." He picked up a pen and tapped it on his desk. "Have you thought about selling?"

I went ramrod in my seat. "No." I gritted my teeth, swallowing down a string of curse words I wanted to fire at the smug prick. "It's just this drought. It can't last much longer. When the rain comes…"

"You can't predict the weather." His lips lifted in a smug little curl. "And if the rain doesn't come?"

"It will." I tucked my hair behind my ear and licked my dry lips. "I hoped you might extend my loan. I just need a few months, then when things get back to normal, and cattle prices go back up, I'll have money coming in. We've also got several horses nearly ready to sell. They'll get a great price. Eli's done such an amazing job with them."

He sat forward in his chair and stared at me. "You're going to fail, Ms. Smith." He darted a glance over my shoulder. "I knew your mother when she still lived here. She was a…a good woman." His stare returned to mine. "Which is why I'm saying this. Get out, get out now, before you lose everything. That ranch is going to fall to pieces with you running it, that's a fact. Sell now and it won't take you down with it."

I sat there staring at him, torn between storming out and hurling his paperweight at him. I wanted to tell him he was wrong, that I'd been in charge of the financial side of running the goddamn ranch for the last five years. But what came out of my mouth was something else entirely. "You knew my mother?"

His face flushed red, and he whipped out his pocket square, dabbing at his top lip. "Of course I did. She used to live in this town."

No. There was more to this, and I had an idea what had caused the bad blood between my dad and this asshole. My stomach churned. "You made it sound like you knew her more than just some passing acquaintance."

His eyes darted away, and he cleared his throat. "I guess

you could say we were…close." He mopped his brow. "We were…friends. And I know she'd hate to see you struggling like this."

"How the hell would you know what she'd think or feel? I certainly don't. That woman hasn't talked to me since she walked out on us."

His assessing stare stayed locked on me, and I wanted to poke him in the goddamn eye. "You look like her, you know." His expression turned appreciative. "That striking blond hair…your figure…"

I shot to my feet. I didn't want to talk about her. I sure as hell didn't like the direction this conversation was going. "Will you give me the three months or not, Mr. Jacobson?"

He snapped his mouth shut. "Well, I…I'll let you know."

Swinging my bag over my shoulder, I forced out a "Thank you" and stormed from his office.

God, had my mother and Connor Jacobson had an affair? Is that why she left, why my parents split up? How could she do that to my dad, to me? Is that why she'd stayed away, a guilty conscience? I shook my head. I didn't care. Not about her, not anymore. The only thing I cared about was keeping my ranch. I'd never sell. Never.

I climbed into the truck, and that bastard's words rang in my ears the whole way home.

He was wrong. I wasn't going to fail.

No goddamn way.

Chapter Six

I finger-combed my hair, still a little damp from the shower, and eyed my wardrobe.

After my appointment with the bank, I'd come home and gotten busy with paperwork. Eli had already been out moving stock from the north field, and when he came in, went off to work with the horses. I'd glimpsed him several times throughout the day but hadn't sought him out. After what happened at the bank, as well as what happened in the barn the day before, I was a little off balance.

Nothing had ever felt as right as the moment he'd thrust his fingers in my hair and demanded I open my mouth. Nothing. A shiver slid through me, my skin getting tingly and tight just from the memory.

When I'd finished for the day and had finally pulled it together enough to talk to him, I couldn't find him. In the end I'd left a note on the pad by the barn door, asking him to come for dinner. I didn't know if he'd seen it, or if he'd come.

I picked a cornflower-blue dress and slipped it on over my head. Hope. That goddamn dangerous emotion bloomed, refusing to be contained. He'd seemed okay...after we...after what happened in the barn. But then he'd left for the night. The thought that he might have left to get away from me stung. A lot.

He'd had time to think everything through, and I was scared he'd change his mind about what we were doing. That thought made my belly churn. I didn't know what I'd do if that happened. Something deeper than sex was developing between us. Every time we were together it grew and shifted, changed shape. I didn't recognize us anymore. It all had changed in such a short time. I didn't know what we were doing, but I did know I didn't want it to stop. I wanted to explore the attraction between us, take it as far as he was willing to go with me.

The kitchen phone rang, and I jogged down the hall to answer it. "Hello."

"Abi, it's me." *Kyle.*

I pulled the phone away from my ear, ready to hang up.

"Please, hear me out," he called, like he could see me.

I had no interest in talking to him whatsoever, but I didn't want him spreading crap about Eli around town, either, so I pressed the phone to my ear. "What do you want?"

"I wanted to apologize for the way I acted... Ya know, getting pushy or whatever. You're hot, babe. I've been panting after you since we were in high school, you gotta know that. I just...things got outta hand."

Asshole. "Fine." It was so far from fine it wasn't funny.

"Fine?"

"You said you wanted to apologize, so apologize."

He was quiet for several seconds. "Shit," he grumbled. "I'm sorry, Abigail."

I wanted to tell him to stick his sorry where the sun doesn't shine, but that wouldn't help my cause.

"So, ah, you gonna give me another shot, babe? Let me

take you out again and show you how sorry I am?"

There was a cockiness to his voice that annoyed the hell out of me. The guy really was an idiot if he thought I'd ever sign up for a repeat of the other night. "I appreciate the apology, but I don't think that's a good idea."

"What?"

"Look, Kyle…the other night, Eli—"

"That psycho fuck!"

I took a calming breath. "You weren't just being pushy, you were being *really* pushy. You scared me, Kyle." I hated to admit that to him, but my pride would have to take a backseat because I wanted him to understand that what Eli had done was Kyle's own damn fault. "Eli knew it; that's why he did what he did."

"You're overexaggerating. Shit, if he hadn't stuck his big dumb nose in, we would've been just fine."

What? Jesus, the man was delusional. "I want you to stop talking crap about him."

"Shit, whatever." He was silent for a couple seconds. "You're not the only hot piece in this town, Abi. But I'm gonna give you some time to cool down, then we'll try this again."

I opened my mouth to tell him to get lost, but he hung up.

I was still fuming after my conversation with Kyle, stomping around the kitchen, when there was a knock at the door. My anger drained away almost instantly, replaced by a good amount of trepidation—I didn't know how Eli was feeling today, if he wanted to continue with what we were doing. But there was also a delicious hum of excitement riding me. It had only been a day, but I missed him.

Tucking my hair behind my ear, I rushed to the door.

I pulled it open, and Eli was standing there. He was fresh from the shower. I could smell the subtle scent of his soap. His jeans and shirt were clean, and his hair still looked damp. I bit my lip at the look in his eyes, the deep flush that crept over his cheeks when he took me in from head to toe in return.

"Got your note," he said softly.

I smiled a wobbly smile. "I didn't know if you'd come… after everything that happened."

He dipped his head and looked at me from under his lashes. "Wasn't you saying those things, Abi. The way I heard it, you were defendin' me." He shook his head. "You don't need to do that, darlin.'"

I wanted to argue with him, but I didn't want to drag all that up again, not when it had caused him pain. So instead I gave him a little nod and pushed the door wider, plastering a bright smile on my face. "I hope you're hungry."

His eyes locked with mine, and his voice turned smoky. "Yes, ma'am."

My belly quivered. "Well, you better come on in then."

I sat him at the kitchen table, gave him a beer, and got on with dishing up. I'd put my favorite tablecloth down. It was a floral print—I loved anything with flowers on it. Seeing Eli sitting there, I was surprised how he looked even more rugged, more masculine against the feminine print.

The steak was done to perfection, juicy and thick. Eli always got the steak when it was on the menu. His favorite, he'd once told me. Well, he hadn't exactly offered that information, but when I'd asked him on our way home from a trip to town, he'd nodded. I grinned to myself as I dished up the potatoes and salad, then put a loaf of freshly baked bread on the table. His gaze followed me as I grabbed our plates, making me tingle all over.

He murmured his thank-you when I put it in front of him, then I sat as well, and we started to eat. Eli did what he always did, tucking into his meal like a man starved…

My potato turned to ash in my mouth. I took a sip of beer. "Is it true?" The words were out of my mouth before I could choke them down with my dinner.

He paused, looking up at me.

"A-about your father…starving you, abusing you."

"Yes."

His voice sounded raw, and it skittered down my spine, my blood starting to boil all over again. "That son of a bitch." Fury vibrated in my voice.

His Adam's apple slid up and down his throat. "Don't think about it, Abigail."

What the hell was wrong with me? He didn't want to talk about this. I'd made him dinner, then dragged up some of the worst memories of his life before he'd even finished. "I'm sorry," I whispered, feeling like an insensitive fool.

He lowered his knife and fork. "Don't pity me, darlin'. I can't take that, not from you." Then he looked back at his dinner and carried on eating.

I didn't know what to say. I ached for him. I didn't pity him. But I'd already jammed my foot far enough down my throat for one night, so I kept my mouth shut.

"Where did you go today?" he asked a few minutes later.

I'd hoped to avoid this conversation, but Eli worked here, so he deserved to know what was going on. "The bank. Things are…they're not great at the moment. I asked Connor Jacobson for a loan extension."

His brow scrunched. "That bad?"

"Yes." Humiliation heated my face. I hated that I was failing. Maybe Connor was right…

"Will the horses cover it?"

The two that were nearly ready for sale would definitely free things up. "Yes, but they're not there yet."

"They're close. I'll have them ready in a week."

"You're putting in enough hours as it is…"

"One week, Abigail. Start looking for buyers."

I was as independent as the next woman. I liked it that

way. But the way he'd said that, the way he made it impossible to doubt him, impossible not to trust that he'd come through for me... God, it made me want to crawl across the table and climb into his lap. He'd taken my troubles on himself instantly and offered up a solution, was willing to put in the extra time, take on the extra work to help me. I think he took a little piece of my heart in that moment.

We ate in silence after that, and despite the conversation we'd had so far, it wasn't uncomfortable. But I was restless—and achy, and going a little bit nuts having him this close and not touching me. The fact that he'd now finished eating and was watching me wasn't helping one goddamn bit, either.

I finally finished, put down my knife and fork, and looked up at him. "Dessert?"

He shifted in his seat, then shook his head.

Was he going to go? I didn't want him to go. I wanted more of what he gave me in the barn.

I didn't mind the silences, but I hated that I didn't know what he was thinking or feeling. Was he as desperate for me as I was for him? I stood and collected our plates, then headed back to the table to grab his empty beer bottle and what was left of the bread. I leaned over the table...

His hand pressed against my lower back and I stilled. Just that, that simple touch—and I was an addict getting a much-needed hit of my favorite drug.

It slid up along my spine until his hand was between my shoulder blades, heat radiating through the fabric of my dress. He touched my hair gently, making my head tingle, then dragged his palm down again, until it rested just above my ass. *Oh God.*

His fingers flexed, dipping farther, and he stilled, making a throaty sound.

He'd discovered my lack of underwear. The heat of that wide, rough palm dropped lower, down to my butt cheek, and he lightly squeezed.

I moaned softly, holding my breath as slowly, ever so slowly, he slid the fabric higher. His breathing had grown choppy, choppier than my own. "You're bare under this pretty dress?"

"Yes." Cool air kissed my thighs, then higher.

"Oh, darlin'," he said huskily.

I squirmed. He was still seated, right there. Could he see how slick my thighs were? How much I wanted him? Then his hand was on me again, this time with nothing between us.

"So pretty," he murmured, then my dress was lifted higher, and the hot press of his lips grazed the base of my spine. Fire shot between my thighs, knees turning to jelly. And the whole time, his hand squeezed and massaged my ass. He continued with the soft kisses, grip firm, holding me where I was, bent over the table, where he wanted me.

I was already wet. Just sitting across the table from him had made me that way. But this...

I started to shake.

"Jesus Christ, Abigail."

He jerked me away from the table suddenly and spun me around. My dress dropped back into place before his hands landed on my hips. He looked up at me as he spread his heavy thighs and drew me closer. Lowering his head, he pressed his face to my belly, then he hefted me higher, ass against the edge of the table, and dipped lower, nose sliding over the thin fabric covering my belly button. His massive arms slid around my waist, and the chair scraped against the floor as he shifted closer, so he could go lower still. The cotton of my dress cupped my mound, hiding nothing, and I whimpered when his nose bumped against it, grabbing for the table behind me so I didn't collapse in a heap.

He ran his nose up and down my slit and drew in a deep breath. A heavy shudder moved through his powerful body, then his tongue darted out, pressing against the thin fabric, grazing my swollen clit through it.

My legs spread wider all on their own, silently asking for more. I was close to losing my mind, I wanted this man so much.

He looked up at me, and there was so much raw hunger there, I couldn't think straight. "Love the way you smell," he rasped. "I want to taste it, darlin'. Will you let me?"

I threaded my fingers through his dark hair, and he moaned, leaning into me like he had that first night in the barn. His fingers were restless against my hips, and there was a desperation in his eyes that, even though it should be impossible, sent my arousal higher. "Yes."

I barely got the word out, and he lifted me higher until I was sitting on the table properly in front of him. The chair scraped again, and he came closer, my legs spreading wider to make room for his wide shoulders.

I was full-on panting when he began sliding my dress up. The slight tremble in his hands, the way he licked his lips, sent my anticipation through the ceiling. My thighs quivered as his roughened palms skated higher, spreading me wider. His eyes were locked on the spot between my thighs, and the dark excitement on his face, the way his nostrils flared when I was fully revealed to him, had me on the verge of coming before he'd even put his mouth on me.

Then he leaned in, pressing his lips to my upper thigh. The scruff covering his jaw lightly scraped my skin, and I was in sensation overload. He rested his cheek there, eyes on my swollen lips as he dragged his other hand higher, then without warning, pressed his thumb deep, sliding the pad over my opening.

I gasped and fought to stay still, to let him explore my body, but right then it was the hardest thing I'd ever done. He slid his thumb up and back several times, spreading my arousal, sliding over my throbbing clit, playing with me, exploring. Then after one more press and slide through my aching lips, he took his thumb away and sucked it into his mouth. His eyes drifted shut, a moan rumbling from his massive chest, and he licked it clean.

His eyes shot open, and his hands went to my hips, fingers digging in a second before he jerked me closer and buried his face between my thighs. I cried out when his mouth made contact with my swollen flesh, when he opened his lips around my entrance and dragged his tongue over me. I fell to my elbows, knocking his empty beer bottle over. He sucked and licked, kissing me like he'd kissed my mouth the day before. His nose bumped my clit, and I whimpered, hand going to his head, fisting his hair, unable to stop myself from grinding against him. He growled, and the sound vibrated through me.

Holy shit.

He tormented me for the longest time, until I was near out of my mind. Then, finally, he pushed a thick finger inside me, his lips wrapping around my clit, sucking at the same time. I hadn't expected it, and fire washed through me. I screamed at the rough, delicious intrusion. My orgasm slamming into me hard and fast. I squeezed my thighs closed around his head, while I arched, rubbing my spasming sex against his face. His hands went to my ass and held me there, eating me like he couldn't get enough, keeping me there, spiraling out of control, at the mercy of his wicked tongue.

Finally I collapsed back, flat on the table, trying to catch my breath. Eli was still between my thighs, gently kissing and licking me, nuzzling my inner thigh, sucking my skin.

When one of his hands left my hip, I mustered the energy to look down my body at him. He'd dropped it between his legs, frantically working his zipper. I couldn't see his cock from my position, but I knew when he'd freed it and started jacking. It was thrilling that putting his mouth on me got him that worked up, that when he was with me like this, he forgot everything but the way I made him feel. But I didn't want him coming in his hand, not this time. I wanted that big cock inside me. I didn't know if he wanted the same thing, if he wanted to go that far, but I found myself tightening my grip in his hair.

"Eli…"

He didn't hear me. Mouth still at my thigh, nuzzling me as he worked himself.

I pushed myself up. "Eli, stop…"

He stilled, eyes lifting to mine, lids hooded, heavy, confused. "Did I… Did I do something…?"

"You did nothing wrong." I quickly added, "You've done everything right." I sat up, steadying myself with one hand on his shoulder, the other cupping his whiskered jaw, and held his hungry gaze. "Do you want to fuck me, Eli?"

He sucked in a rough breath through his nose. "Yes," he said instantly. The dark hunger I saw in him intensified. Jesus, I'd never been this hot for anyone, not ever. "But are you… are you sure?"

I slid my thumb over his bottom lip, and though he'd stopped stroking his cock, I noticed the way he squeezed his fist around the wide base, the way his mouth parted when he did. His tongue darted out, tasting my skin, and I shivered. "I want you inside me, Elijah." Sliding off the table, forcing him to sit back, I grabbed the bottom of my dress and dragged it over my head. "Badly."

His hand dropped away from his cock, and he leaned back, inviting me to climb onto his lap. His scent wrapped around me, the sound of his ragged breaths. I moved between his thighs and pulled off his shirt, tossing it aside, then climbed on, straddling him. His chest was pumping rapidly, his breaths shaky and harsh.

"Okay?"

He nodded, his hands going to my waist.

The crisp hair on his chest abraded my nipples, making them tighten to aching peaks, and the impressive ridge of his cock dragged over my bare flesh. I groaned and slid my arms around his neck. "I love the way you feel pressed up against me like this," I whispered, trembling with how much I wanted him. I touched his face, my fingers on his cheek, thumb sliding over his chin, and leaned in to kiss him. One of his arms banded around me instantly, lips meeting mine without hesitation. I opened my mouth over his, sliding my tongue inside. He groaned, then he was kissing me back. Deep licks, fucking my mouth. He growled when I sucked his tongue, his hand dropping to my ass, squeezing hard enough to hurt but instead it felt so damn good. He held me there, the underside of his cock spreading me, grinding against me, grazing my clit.

He kissed my chin, my throat. "Darlin'," he rasped against my neck. "Please...please...I can't..." He hissed, humping against me. "I want inside, let me inside, sweetheart."

Every word this man said had the ability to destroy me. His honesty blew me away. Eli didn't play games; he said what he felt, and I could deny him nothing.

I reached down, fisted his cock, and using his shoulder as leverage, pulled myself up. Positioning the head at my opening, I wrapped both arms around his neck and lowered myself slowly. The fat head breached my opening, and I bit my lip. *Oh shit*. He was hot and hard and so damn thick.

He bucked, a shout exploding past his lips. Gripping my hips, he thrust up, slamming me down at the same time, filling me to the root, like he'd reached the edge of his control and flown over.

I cried out and dug my nails into his shoulders. He was so damn big, stretching me to my limits. I dropped my head to his chest, breathing through it, the pleasure-pain firing through me. That's when I realized he'd gone completely still. Apart from his chest and the pounding of his heart against mine, he was like stone beneath me. I lifted my head, and his eyes were screwed shut, teeth gritted.

"Eli?"

"I'm hurting you." He shook his head. "I've never done this before… I've never…and I'm hurting you."

Oh God.

"Look at me." His eyes opened, and what I saw nearly killed me. The man was so damn conflicted, and hating himself for it. I placed my hands on his shoulders, fingers brushing the side of his neck, and circled my hips.

He exhaled heavily on a low moan, his massive, sinewy body rolling up to meet mine. "I can't… I can't stop…"

"I don't want you to." I leaned in and kissed him gently. "You're so big, Elijah. I just needed a minute to adjust. But you feel so good. The sweetest ache I've ever felt."

He licked his lips, biceps jumping under my searching hands. "Couldn't bear it if I hurt you."

"You didn't hurt me. Can't you feel how wet I am?" I circled my hips again.

He cursed. "And tight, darlin'. So goddamn tight."

Grinding down, I gasped when he went deeper and tightened my arms around his neck so I could rock against him. "Feels good, doesn't it? Only you do that to me. Only you make me this way."

With how I was straddling him, my feet unable to touch the ground, all I could do was move my hips against his, grinding and rocking. We both needed more. I kissed him. "Lift me," I whispered against his lips. "Use me. Use me to get off." I rolled my hips again. "Fuck me, Eli."

"God, you want that, don't you, Abigail?" Those big, rough hands cupped my ass. "You want me to fuck you, take you?"

I tried to move my hips, but he was holding me still. "Please."

He snapped then, a growl exploding from him, and he lifted me effortlessly, bringing me back down. We both groaned.

I didn't need to give him instruction after that because he took over, took what he wanted, bringing me down on his massive dick over and over until I was a mindless, shaking mess. His heavy stare never left mine once, watching me, growing more intense, wilder. We were slick with sweat, panting, grinding, kissing.

I couldn't take it another minute, and at the same time never wanted it to end. My climax was hovering just out of reach, teetering on the edge. I grabbed one of his hands and pressed his fingers to my clit. "Rub it, please. Please let me come."

He did what I asked. Rough-skinned fingers expertly sliding over my slippery, swollen clit. "Do you need me to take you there, beautiful girl?"

At his question, my sex started pulsing. I whimpered, using his shoulders again to keep us sliding against each other, while he continued to work me.

I knew he could feel it, because his expression turned fierce. "That's it. Come around my cock, Abigail."

He'd never said anything like that before; hell, he'd never said my name like that before, and for some reason, that's what tipped me over the edge. That gritty voice, filled with sex and need, saying my name.

I screamed and rode him through it. His hand moved from between my legs and returned to my hips, then he took control again, slamming me down and at the same time thrusting up into me. He began to shake and groan, cock pulsing relentlessly as his hot come shot deep inside me, setting off wave after wave of exquisite aftershocks.

When he was done, I dropped my head forward, resting it on his shoulder. His hand was on my back, that fine sandpaper skin of his moving over mine, making me tingle all over.

Turning my face to the side, I tilted back, looking up at him, feeling more nurtured and cared for in that moment, in Eli's arms, than I ever had. Running his fingers through my hair, brushing it away from my face, he stared down at me.

"Was it how you imagined?" I whispered.

He shook his head and pressed fingers lightly over the rapidly beating pulse at my neck. "So much better."

I knew I was smiling like crazy, but I didn't even try to hold it in. And as much as I wanted to stay where I was, we couldn't sit like this all night. "Do you want to shower with me?"

"Yes." He instantly lifted me, standing me on my feet.

I looked up, and Eli's gaze was locked on his come sliding down my thighs. I was on the pill and I'd never had sex without a condom before. I probably should have told him that before I climbed into his lap, but neither one of us had been thinking clearly.

"It's okay," I said gently. "I'm on the pill. I'm clean. And since you've never…"

He got up from the chair in a heartbeat, lifting me off the ground and swinging me into his arms. Before I could open my mouth to ask what was going on, his mouth slammed down on mine. He kissed me hard, tongue tangling with mine.

With a groan, he lifted his head. "I want to fuck you again, Abigail. And I want to watch my come slide down your legs every time I do."

Chapter Seven

The first rays of light filtered into my room, casting patterns on our bare skin through my old lace curtains. Eli was behind me, the tip of his finger gently tracing the shadowed flower design on my hip. That's how I woke. Neither of us had said a word. I didn't even know if he knew I was awake...

Just the thought of last night, the kitchen, the shower, then here in this bed had my pulse quickening and heat growing between my legs. I'd never felt this way about another person before—I couldn't describe it. There was this unwavering lust that constantly pounded through me. I craved him all the time. And yet I'd never been more content, even with all my troubles. His body behind mine, his scent, his warmth, the sound of his steady breaths... I could stay like this forever. I wanted to let him take care of me, and I wanted to take care of him in return. I didn't have a name for it...was too afraid to try...not yet...

My tummy rumbled loudly.

Elijah stilled behind me, then a second later, he removed his hand from my hip and rolled away. His feet thudded against the floor.

I twisted to look at him and almost bit my tongue. Elijah Hays was the most exquisite man I'd ever seen in jeans and a T-shirt, but naked? Dear God, he was magnificent. Tall and broad, rippling muscle and rugged angles. The definition of masculine. He was striding away, his back and bare ass on full display as he headed for the bedroom door.

I finally got my mouth to work. "Where are you going?"

He stopped, rested a hand on the doorframe, and looked at me. "Wait there, Abigail." He said it gently, but there was no mistaking the command behind it.

Did he know he was doing it? Issuing those quiet orders? Was he aware of the dominant side of himself? Had it always been there? Or had this new development between us brought it out in him? I had no idea why it affected me so damn much. Why that gentle order, given with that gritty rasp, low and deep, turned my belly to warm liquid, had me lying here eager for his return.

I heard him banging around in the kitchen, and it was hard not to go and see what he was doing, but I did as he said and waited right there. He was back ten minutes later. I hadn't even heard him coming. You'd think with the size of the man that would be impossible. He was carrying a mug and a plate. His gaze swept over me as he neared the bed, and his eyes glittered in a satisfied way that sent a jolt of pleasure through me. He placed the mug on the small table beside me, then put the plate on my lap. There were two slices of toast with Cassie's homemade blueberry jam spread on it.

My heart did a little flutter as I scooched up the bed. "You made me breakfast?"

"You're hungry," he said simply and climbed in beside me.

I brushed my hair away from my face. "Yeah, but you didn't need to do that. I could've—" My belly rumbled again, loudly.

His whole body went tense. "Eat the toast, darlin'."

I picked up a piece and took a bite. It didn't take a genius to work out what this was about, why he'd reacted this way. If me being hungry caused him distress, brought back memories that caused him pain, I'd eat the damn toast. His entire body seemed to relax as I chewed.

I'd finished half of the first piece and washed it down with tea before I spoke. "How did you know I like tea and not coffee?"

He lifted a hand, sliding it up my thigh. My breath hitched. "Same way I know you only wear your beautiful blond hair down when we go to town, or after your shower in the evening. Same way I know you're afraid of storms and that you love to dance." He continued higher, to the dip in my waist, then up until he was skimming the underside of my breast. "I pay attention. When it comes to you, I've always paid attention." He looked up at me. "Please, keep eating."

Oh God. Who was this man? What was he doing to me?

He watched me finish the first piece. I took another sip of tea, then picked up the second. I could've stopped after that one slice, but having all of his attention on me was too addictive. I found I wanted to please him, and if that meant eating another piece of toast, I would. I also loved the way he was touching me while he watched. He was lying on his side, eyes on my lips, moving over my face, and his hand never stopped petting me, teasing me. I was tingling all over, goose bumps prickling my skin. Like a contented cat, desperate for another stroke from her master.

I shivered, not sure how that made me feel. Eli had sneaked up on me. Everything about him was a surprise. And every small piece of himself he revealed just made me hunger for more.

"You don't like it when I'm hungry?" I said into the silence.

He shook his head.

I thought I knew, but I wanted him to open up, just a little, to share some of that burden with me. "Why?" I whispered.

He didn't look at me. Instead he watched his hand, following the path it took over my skin. "Being hungry hurts," he rasped, then lifted his eyes to mine. "Don't ever want you to hurt, Abigail."

Tears immediately stung the backs of my eyes. "I'm so sorry, Elijah."

"Don't...don't pity me, Abigail." He shook his head. "Not you."

He'd said that to me before, and it killed me he thought I felt that way. "I don't pity you. I feel..." I released a shaky breath, trying to release some of the anger suddenly surging through me. "I feel fucking furious that you had to go through that, that half this shitty town knew and did nothing."

His hand stilled on my hip, and his fingers flexed, pressing into my skin, something new and beautiful transforming his rugged face. "I'm okay, darlin'," he said roughly.

In some ways, yes, he was more than okay. But my belly had barely rumbled, and he'd bolted out of bed to get me food, like the sheets were on fire. He would've been very young when he became aware of the abuse in his home. His mother must have suffered at the hands of his bastard father for a lot of years before Eli was old enough to do something about it. I got the feeling that's where this need to take care of me came from. Did he believe he'd failed her in some way?

"Is it true? Did you kill him?" I could barely believe I'd said it out loud, but I realized as soon as I did that the answer didn't matter to me. It never had.

His eyes lifted to mine, held, and I could see him physically brace himself. "Yes."

"Good," I rasped.

His entire body quaked. "Good?"

"You had to protect yourself and your mom. No one else was doing it. You did the only thing you could."

"Christ, darlin'." He dropped his head to my lap, wrapping his arms around my legs, and I ran my fingers through his rumpled hair. We didn't talk anymore about that. We didn't need to. It changed nothing, not for me.

Instead we talked about the ranch, plans to get things back on track, what I'd make for dinner that night. If he wanted to share more with me, I'd be here, but I wasn't going to push.

I still had half a piece of toast left, but I'd had enough. "I'm full," I said, and he lifted his head.

I held it to his lips. He obviously believed me, because he bit it in half. I handed him my tea and watched him finish it off. Even the way he ate was appealing, the way the muscles in his jaw jumped when he chewed. Damn, it was sexy.

He finished the drink, then handed the cup to me to put on the side table. He shifted closer then, leaning over me, taking me to my back, one hand on the mattress at my side, the other lifting to my jaw. He touched me with such tenderness my heart squeezed. Those fingers skimmed my throat, my breasts. He cupped one, holding it in a grip that could only be described as possessive, and squeezed, swiping his thumb over the hard peak until I was panting. He kept going, trailing the coarse, callused tips of his fingers over my quivering belly. The expression on his face, the way he touched me, it was like I was uncharted territory and he was discovering every dip, curve, and valley for the first time.

"I like knowing you're full. It makes me feel"—he looked like he was struggling to find the right words—"full as well, but in a different way. It's hard to explain." He slid farther down my body and gripped my thighs, spreading them, exposing my bare sex to his hungry gaze.

I whimpered, his words swirling through my head mixed with the way he was affecting my body. I didn't know which way was up. Just his eyes on me, his voice sliding over me, had me squirming.

He moved between my legs and dropped lower. "Only thing I'm hungry for is you." Nuzzling my inner thigh, he spread me open with his fingers, and I watched him suck in a sharp breath, his eyes glazing over. "You like the way my hands feel on you?" His voice had gotten rougher.

He slid his fingers through my drenched slit, and I arched against the mattress. "Yes."

"I like having you all over me. The way you smell. The way you taste." He groaned, nose gliding higher up my thigh. "Ah, you're soaking, Abi. So wet. I do that to you, don't I, sweetheart? You get this way because of the way I touch you?"

I was trembling, thigh muscles twitching. "Yes." I reached down and threaded my fingers in his sleep-rumpled hair. "Please, Eli. I need your mouth on me."

He growled, wrapped his hands around my thighs, and buried his face between my legs. His deep moan as he dragged his nose through my slick lips, covering himself in me, had me trying to grind against him. I didn't get very far, though; those strong hands held me immobile, held me tight against his mouth. And dear God, the sounds he made, the pleasure he was taking from going down on me, was one of the hottest things I'd ever experienced.

He lapped and sucked, growling as he worked me. It was so damn good. My moans were constant now, filling the room. I learned last night, the last few days, the man knew how to make me come, which meant he was purposely holding off. "Please, Eli," I begged, and tightened my grip on his hair. "Let me come, baby. Please let me come."

He pulled back, and I could see the satisfaction in his eyes. The man loved it when he made me beg. He lifted his mouth away, and I cried out, ready to beg all over again, but then he replaced his lips and tongue with his fingers. His head dropped to my inner thigh, getting a close-up view of my quivering sex. I loved watching him like this. He circled my clit like I'd shown him, making me writhe and buck. "More?" he asked, warm breath tickling my damp skin.

I bucked. "More."

He continued to circle my clit, then dipped down, spreading more of my arousal, then up again. Rubbing back and forth over the sensitive bundle of nerves. He leaned in and lapped at my opening, again and again—then he pushed his tongue inside me and I shattered. Crying out, body shaking. And somehow through my haze, I heard Eli's groan of approval.

I was still spasming when his tongue slid over my sensitive flesh, lapping up my come. His hands gripped my butt, and he spread my cheeks, swiping down the crease, getting every drop. I shuddered and spread my legs wider for him. He paused, just for a second, then he was at my ass. He circled my puckered hole with his tongue, up and back, groaning the whole time.

Nerves kicked up in my belly, blended with excitement. How the hell could I still want more after the orgasm he'd just given me? But that's what Eli did to me.

God, it was so good, all of it. Everything he did to me made me wet and achy.

He licked and sucked me, played with me until I was swollen and aching and wet again. I was getting restless, desperate. I needed him inside me, and he obviously felt the same way, because he rose up, and after wiping his face on the sheet, positioned himself over me.

His cock jutted from his huge, muscled body, long and so damn hard. Thick veins bulged along the length, and the tip was dark. Jesus, I wanted him. I spread my legs wider, inviting him to take me. My skin was burning up, slick, and I was close to undulating on the bed. I was that desperate for him.

His expression was all heat...fierce. "I need inside you again, Abigail," he said. "Will you let me fuck you, sweetheart?" Despite the possessiveness in his eyes, the way he touched me, there were still these traces of uncertainty. He was still questioning what was happening between us. How much I wanted him.

I'd never seen that look on his face before, had never heard that sweet, hungry edge to his voice. Didn't he know he didn't have to ask? I was dying for him. "You can have me, Eli. You can have me any time you want me."

His nostrils flared, and he growled as he dropped down, covering my body with his—and before I had the chance to start begging again, the fat head of his cock was stretching me open, sliding in an inch.

"Is this mine, Abi?" He lifted up onto his hands and stared down at me.

I gripped his ass, digging my nails into firm muscle. "Yes... yes, it's yours."

His eyes flashed, and he slammed forward, filling me in one brutal thrust.

"Oh shit," I cried. "That feels so good, Eli. You feel so good."

His body strained above me, every muscle bunched, every vein and tendon bulging under his tanned skin. His hips were slamming into mine, over and over, the wet slap of our skin, our harsh breaths filling my head.

He growled. "Oh God, sweetheart...I need...I want..." he started, then stopped himself, gritting his teeth.

I opened my mouth to tell him to take whatever he wanted, but I didn't need to. I saw the moment he decided that for himself. His eyes got hotter, darker, the fierceness moving to a whole new level. A moment later he pulled out, gripped my hips, and flipped me onto my stomach. He arranged me how he wanted me, no asking for permission this time. He lifted my ass in the air, then he rammed into me from behind, taking me how he wanted.

I screamed, biting my pillow. He was big, but from behind, even more so, stretching me to almost the point of pain. The kind of burn that only made the pleasure I was already experiencing that much better. I must have freaked him out, because he stopped, cock buried inside me, fingers digging into my hips.

I couldn't make my mouth work to tell him I was okay, so I did the only thing I could, I fucked back onto him, telling him what I wanted without words, taking him deeper.

He barked a curse, then he was drilling into me again.

He hit me deep, and I was coming, my walls clamping down on him so damn hard I knew I wouldn't be the only one seeing stars. He gritted out a rough sound, and still gripping my hips, began fucking me without restraint, powering that huge cock into me, over and over, until I was crying and shaking, clawing at the sheets.

I came twice more before he finally pulled me down onto his cock with force and roared his release, pumping me so full of his come that it was sliding out of me before he'd finished.

When he pulled out, he collapsed to the side, taking me with him. Then he rolled me onto my back, brushed my hair off my face, and stared down at me. He was puffing, his massive chest heaving. I lay limp, like my bones had dissolved.

"Are you okay? I didn't hurt you?"

I managed to shake my head.

His brow creased. "Did I make you feel good, darlin'?"

I'd have thought he was joking, if it weren't for his serious expression.

I couldn't help it. I wrapped my fingers around the side of his neck, pulled him down so his face was buried against my throat, and giggled uncontrollably, managing between gasped breaths to get out, "If it'd been any better, I'd be unconscious."

That's when I heard it for the first time, that deep, low sound that cut off my giggles and had my heart growing bigger, so big I didn't know how it was still beating.

Elijah Hays was laughing, and it was the most beautiful thing I'd ever heard.

Chapter Eight

I parked the tractor in front of the barn and jumped down. The feed was getting low, there was no sign of rain, and I still hadn't heard from Connor Jacobson about the loan extension. It had only been a few days, I guess, but I got the impression he wasn't in any hurry to help me out, not after that conversation in his office.

Asshole.

Short of stripping and doing a rain dance, I wasn't sure what the hell I could do.

I walked around the side of the tractor and toward the training pen...and nearly tripped over my own two feet. Ever since I told him about my troubles with the bank, Eli had upped his training schedule with the horses. The mare was doing really well, and I knew without a doubt she'd bring in a pretty penny. Not just as a cow horse, either. She came from good stock, and if her new owner wanted to get her in foal, those foals would bring top dollar. It's something my dad and I had wanted to do for as far back as I could remember, but we never quite got there. Not when there were bills waiting to be paid. The short-term turnaround always took precedence. It was how we'd kept this place going. Dad, like Eli, had had a way with horses. The two of them, both training and selling, had allowed us to keep this place afloat. Obviously things had slowed after his death, and as happy I was that Eli was helping me out of the bind I found myself in, I didn't want him blaming himself or working himself into the ground.

Right now he was on his own horse. Gus was a gentle giant like his owner, and his unruffled nature was perfect in the training pen. The mare was giving him the odd sideways glance, but she wasn't frightened or dancing away when Eli rode near. She was doing great, had come so far in such a short time.

But what had me tripping and stumbling over my boots was the way Eli looked in the saddle. It never got old. He was born to it.

I headed over, the flutter in my belly increasing the closer I got. His jeans and boots were covered in dust, and his blue T-shirt was plastered to his chest and abs as he rode in a wide circle. He'd turned his cap backward, so I could see his face clearly, the way his lips moved as he talked to his horse, the lines crinkling the corners of his eyes when he gently smiled, pleased with something they did. That smile, small as it was, was breathtaking.

But it wasn't just his smile. It was the whole package. The last few nights we'd spent together had been life-altering. He was still a little unsure, not always trusting his instincts. I was doing everything I could to let him know how amazing he was, that nothing he wanted from me was wrong. But he was still holding back, afraid of what he wanted, maybe afraid that I'd reject him if he took what he needed…and I knew he craved more. I sensed it in him so strongly, it was like I could see inside him. I didn't know how to convince him to let go, other than telling him how much I loved everything he did to me.

I trusted him with my body completely. His size, his quiet nature, his past and fears, none of that could hide his beautiful soul.

He'd never hurt me. Ever.

I leaned on the fence and watched him, unable to look away. I wanted him, now. Constantly. And when he lifted his head and spotted me, and that dark, dirty heat sliced through his brown eyes, I knew he felt the same way. His mouth quirked up on one side, gaze roaming my body, and the hot needy sensations it caused shot through me, rippling over my skin. He adjusted his ass in the saddle, and I grinned. The man was now sporting wood, and we both knew there was nothing he could do about it, not right then.

I was in the mood to be a little naughty, to tease. So I leaned over the railing farther. My tank was low cut, and I pushed my arms together, giving him a nice view of cleavage down the front. His brows shot up and then lowered, eyes narrowing. I threw him a wink, then after I'd flashed him once more, I gave him a little wave, turned and, adding an extra sway to my hips, walked away.

I probably shouldn't tease, but it was all in fun, and the more worked up Eli got, the more control he let slip. There was a raging inferno inside that man just waiting to be released.

And I wanted him to release it on me.

I headed inside. I didn't have long to get ready before Cassie came to pick me up. There had been a fair in town today, and they were having a live band tonight. I'd said I'd go before Eli and I had gotten together. I'd mentioned it to him yesterday, but I knew he wouldn't come. I would've backed out, but I'd agreed to meet an old school friend of mine who was in town for a few days and I didn't want to let him down. We barely saw each other anymore as it was, and I missed him. James had been my best friend since the third grade. When we got older, we'd tried dating. It hadn't worked out, but we never stopped being friends, and I hoped we always would be.

I grabbed a quick shower and got dressed, leaving my hair loose and putting on my favorite dress. It was still hot, even when the sun went down, so I didn't bother with a sweater. Eli was just finishing up when I walked out, leading Gus toward me from the field. He'd spun his cap around again, so I couldn't see his eyes as he neared, but I didn't miss the way his massive shoulders had stiffened or how the bulge in the front of his jeans had grown.

He stopped in front of me, and I patted Gus's nose. He nudged my hand, greedy for more pats.

"Cassie should be here soon."

Eli's face was still in shadow, and I sucked in a breath when he reached out and touched my waist, hand smoothing over the rose-print fabric.

"Do you like it?"

"You look beautiful." His hand lifted to my hair, touching the ends, then across to my jaw, the side of my throat. "Beautiful," he said again in a gruff voice.

The sound of Cassie's truck coming up the road reached us, and he dropped his hand.

"I won't be too late."

He dipped his chin and led Gus to the fence to brush him down.

Cassie pulled up beside us, casting a glance in Eli's direction. He murmured, "Hello," and got on with what he was doing. Cassie seemed to relax after that. I don't know what she thought he'd do, but it annoyed the hell out of me that she was so wary of him in the first place. I tried not to think about it. Tonight I planned on having a good time.

"Is James meeting you there, honey?" Cassie asked. "I saw him in town yesterday. Boy said he planned to wear you out on the dance floor."

Eli stilled, going full-on statue. *Shit.* James was just my friend; there was nothing romantic between us — not anymore; there barely had been when we dated — but Eli had lived in this town his whole life as well. He had to know that James and I had gone out. I wanted to explain to him, but Cassie had her eagle eyes on me, and as much as I loved her, I had no intention of sharing my and Eli's relationship with her, not yet anyway.

I tried to laugh it off. "I'm sure he'll be too busy sweet-talking the ladies to worry about his old *friend*." I couldn't make it any plainer than that.

Cassie laughed and joked with me as we climbed in her truck, but Eli hadn't moved. His head was tilted down and to the side, that blasted hat hiding his eyes so I couldn't even try to read what he was thinking.

Then we were driving down the road, headed for town. We'd barely left and I was already desperate to get home again, to make sure Eli knew he had nothing to worry about.

When we arrived the band was already playing. The stalls and tents from the fair that day were still up but closed for the night. They'd been arranged in a large circle, a makeshift stage for the band at one end, dancing and mingling in the middle. Decorations and lanterns had been strung up as well, and they cast a soft, warm golden glow across everyone. It was beautiful. I wished Eli were there with me.

I spotted James at the same time he did us.

He rushed over and pulled me into a tight hug. "About time you got here, woman." Then he grabbed my hand and dragged me away from Cassie. "Let's dance."

I laughed. "I just got here. I need a beer first."

"Bullshit." He snorted. "Abigail Smith doesn't need Dutch courage to shake her ass on the dance floor."

Half an hour later we were still there. James was a great dancer, always had been. He spun me around the floor, that wicked glint in his eyes, purposely ignoring the scores of females desperate for his attention. By the time we'd finished another dance or two, he'd have every available woman throwing herself at him—and some that weren't available.

The song changed to a slow one, and he tugged me in close, wrapping his arms around me.

I grinned up at him. "You'll start a catfight soon if you don't start sharing yourself around."

He shrugged. "I don't get to spent time with my best friend very often. They can dance with someone else." He gave me a squeeze. "You seeing anyone, Abi?"

I blinked up at him. He never asked about my love life, not since we had our ill-fated attempt at one. "Why do you ask?" I tried to sound light and breezy, but my belly squirmed at the look in his eyes.

He glanced away, then down at me. "We weren't that bad together, were we?"

I jolted and stared up at him. "Where the hell is this coming from?"

"I don't know." His brow scrunched, and he rubbed the back of his neck like he wasn't quite sure himself. "I've been thinking about coming home." He touched my hair at the side of my face. "You're what I think about when I think about home, I guess."

I gave his arm a light slap. "I love you, you know I do. But we were terrible together." I snickered. "Kissing me was like kissing your sister, and you damn well know it."

The lines at the corners of his eyes crinkled, then he barked out a laugh. "Shit, it was bad, wasn't it?"

"The worst."

He mock shuddered. "Right, forget I ever mentioned it, and let's go get a beer. I feel the urge to get wasted."

He slung an arm over my shoulder and led me to the beer tent, leaving me to wait while he got us drinks. I snorted to myself when he was swarmed as soon as he hit the bar. I may not get hot under the collar for the guy, but I wasn't blind, either. James was a good-looking guy. He was also funny, and if Kasey Cooper was right, a mountain lion in the sack. He was grade-A beef for this pack of husband hunters.

I was still chuckling to myself when I spotted Connor Jacobson a little ways away. I caught James's eye and pointed outside. He gave me a nod, then carried on fighting off his tipsy fan club.

"Mr. Jacobson?" He turned at the sound of his name, eyes moving over me in a way that could only be described as appreciative. My skin crawled.

"Abigail," he said too loudly.

His face was rosy, eyes on the droopy side. The man was hammered.

"Nice to see you, real nice." He rubbed his hand over his mouth.

Jesus. "Sorry," I muttered. "This isn't the time to discuss business." I turned to leave, but he grabbed my arm.

"Now, now, don't go rushing off, honey."

This was going downhill fast. I needed to get away from this creep before he said something that could screw things up for me in a big way. I searched the crowd in the beer tent for James, but he was still surrounded by cooing females.

"I've been thinking…"

Never a good idea.

"You have a predicament." He shuffled a little closer. "Maybe old Con can help you out of your mess."

Old Con? What the hell? "I'm going to stop you right there, Mr. Jacobson. Unless you're going to tell me the bank has agreed to extend my loan, I can't imagine any other way you could help me out."

His eyes glazed over, then he stepped closer. "Your mama and me, we used to get on real good. I think you and me would rub together just as well."

I wrenched my arm out of his hold, sick to my stomach. I didn't bother with a reply. He was too drunk to listen anyway. I just hoped like hell he was drunk enough to forget he'd propositioned me *and* all but admitted to an affair with my mother, or I was screwed.

I spun away from him and collided with a very big, very warm, very familiar chest. I looked up, and my mouth dropped open. "Eli?"

He wasn't looking at me; his scary hostile gaze was locked on my bank manager, and he did not look happy. Not one bit.

I placed my hand on his forearm. "Don't," I whispered. "He's not worth it, let's just…walk away."

James chose that moment to join us, brow hiked to his hairline. "What's going on?"

Elijah turned his scowl on my best friend, and James frowned, then scowled back.

"Okay. Let's go." I planted my hand against Elijah's hard abs and tried to guide him to leave with me. He didn't move. "I asked Eli to come pick me up," I lied. "Cassie's having fun and I have a headache…so…"

James stared. "I would've given you a ride home."

"I didn't want to spoil everyone's fun." I gave Eli another shove. "Can you take me home now?" Finally, he dropped his chin and looked at me. He had his cap on, but I was standing right in front of him and had no trouble seeing his eyes. They were dark, searing into me in a way that made me shiver — in a very good way.

I forced a smile and waved to Cassie, pointing to Eli, so she knew I had a ride home. She frowned as well. Jesus.

"All right," James said, expression suspicious as hell. "I'll give you a call tomorrow?"

"Sounds good." Then I was striding away, hoping like hell Elijah was following me and not still standing there shooting death glares at every male in the vicinity. The man had a light tread, and I didn't know for sure that he was behind me until we cleared the tents and stalls and were heading into the field where everyone had parked their cars. Where the sound of the band had drifted into the distance and the chirp of crickets now filled the night.

That's when his arm snaked around my waist, and he spun me around.

Backing me up, he pressed me against a truck, cold steel seeping through my dress, a towering giant crowding me, his body flush against mine. I was instantly turned on. "Eli..." I started.

He shook his head. "I didn't like that. I didn't like any of it." His grip on my waist tightened. "You look so beautiful." He touched my hair resting over my shoulder. "I don't blame them for wanting you...every man there wanted you. But I didn't like it, Abigail." He released a rough breath. "I don't want anyone touching you but me."

A quiver started low in my belly. "James is just my friend. I promise that's all we are."

His jaw tightened, and I knew he didn't believe me. He confirmed it when he said, "He wants you." His hand slid down to my hip, and he gave me a gentle squeeze. "Do you want him?"

I was shaking my head before he'd finished talking. "No. He's like a brother to me." I placed my hand over his. "As for that sleaze Connor—"

He growled, and his hand went to my ass. "Don't say his name. Don't even mention that bastard to me, not with the way I'm feeling right now."

He pulled away suddenly, grabbed my hand, and started through the cars again. When we got to his truck, he opened the door for me, and I climbed in.

As we left the fairgrounds, I didn't ask him why he'd

come, why he'd shown up, because I already knew. He'd made it damn obvious. He didn't want anyone else touching me, couldn't bear the thought of it.

"How long were you there?" I said into the silent cab, turning to look at him.

His nostrils flared. "I saw you dancing." He was stiff in his seat. "Watched him pull you in close, put his hands on your waist, touch your hair."

"Eli," I whispered, not sure what to say, how to reassure him.

"Didn't like the way that made me feel, darlin'. Not one goddamn bit." His jaw was hard again. "Seeing him run his hands over your body made me want to…" He squeezed the steering wheel. "Made me want to drag you off that damn dance floor and…"

My heart was thudding like crazy in my chest. "And what? What did you want to do?"

He spun to me, fire burning from his eyes. "Punish you for making me feel that way," he snarled. "Bend you over and punish you with my hard cock until my balls are covered in you and you know exactly who your pussy belongs to, that I am the only man with the right to touch you, hold you, comfort you. Me. Only me."

His words sliced through me, and my nipples tightened painfully. My sex was fluttering and swollen, and so damn wet. I started to tremble with the strength of my need.

"Punish me," I whispered into the shadowy cab.

His head shot around to face me. "You don't mean that," he rasped, chest pumping. He shook his head. "I shouldn't have…I never should have said it…I…"

"Punish me," I said again. "Please, I want you to punish me."

"Abi…" He shook his head again, gripping the wheel tighter, so tight it groaned.

I reached out, took one of his hands off the wheel and slid closer, bringing it up under my dress. I spread my legs and placed his hand on my soaked underwear. He had no idea. No idea how much I wanted it. This was the only way I knew to get that across, to let him feel it for himself. "I mean it," I said, voice shaky with lust. "I want it."

He pulled his hand away, and I whimpered, desperate for him, but then he was pulling off the side of the road, taking the dirt track to the old mill. It'd closed fifteen years ago. Nothing was down here anymore, except a secluded spot in the middle of nowhere, and a lake that kids swam in during summer.

"What are you doing?" I asked breathlessly, though I thought I knew, and it turned me on so damn much it was a struggle not to put my hand down the front of my underwear and relieve the ache.

He looked at me again. "I'm going to punish you, Abigail, for letting someone touch what's mine."

Chapter Nine

He drove to the end of the road and kept going until we reached the lake, where he pulled over. It was dark down here, but I could still see the plants, trees, and shrubs surrounding the water's edge, unaffected by the drought.

My heart was hammering when Eli finally turned to me.

"Out, Abi."

I swallowed, trying to get some moisture in my suddenly dry mouth. "Where do you want me?" I could see his control slipping, that molten heat, that dark, dirty part of him creeping forward. At my question, I got a flash of white teeth—not from a smile; no, he was the wolf and I was Little Red Riding Hood.

He gripped the wheel tighter. "Back...go to the back of the truck and stand there."

I could see him fighting it, and as much as telling me what he wanted turned him on, it frightened him as well. This was uncharted territory for both of us, but neither of us was going to back out. We'd been building toward this moment from the first night he'd touched me—maybe even before.

His cock was a thick, hard ridge under the denim of his jeans, begging for my mouth, to be inside me. He was getting off on this as much as I was.

I climbed out and walked to the back of the truck, nervous excitement firing through my belly, and waited. It was cooler down here by the lake, the insects louder, and I could hear leaves rustling in the light breeze. It was idyllic, peaceful—yet none of it quieted the riot going on inside me.

It was only a few seconds, but it seemed like forever before Elijah climbed out and strode toward me, all big, heaving, aroused male.

He stopped beside me, dropped the tailgate, then tugged his shirt off and spread it on the bare steel. His breath was choppy, color high on his cheeks. "Take off the dress."

I did what he asked immediately, lifting it over my head and flinging it into the bed of the truck.

He eyed my bra and panties. "Naked."

I shivered at his rough command and stripped them off as well, putting them with my dress. His body shook, fingers curling and uncurling at his sides. The sun had dropped, but the moon was big and bright, and I could see the way his eyes glittered. The deep hunger there.

He closed the distance between us, towering over me. "Spread your legs."

His voice was filled with anticipation, fueling my already out-of-control need. I stepped out, doing as he asked, and his hand was there before my next breath, middle finger sliding through my swollen lips.

He groaned. "This all for me, darlin'?"

"Yes."

"No one makes you this wet but me. Isn't that right, Abigail?"

He kept up his torment, rubbing that wide, rough finger across my drenched opening, teasing me, not pushing in like

I desperately needed him to. "No one," I said, voice shaky as hell.

He didn't move closer. The only part of him touching me was that maddening finger, tormenting me, making me crazy. "You look so beautiful in the moonlight," he whispered. "Like an angel."

His gaze raked over me, hungry eyes taking me in.

"Does my angel want me to bend her over and punish her with my cock?"

My inner muscles spasmed, and Eli felt it. He forced a breath out through his teeth and came closer, taking one of my breasts in his hand and squeezing.

"You won't let anyone else touch you like that again, will you, darlin'? Like James was touching you?"

I gasped out a breath, shaking my head. "N-no."

His finger vanished, and he spun me before I knew what was happening. His hand pressed between my shoulder blades, and he bent me forward over the tailgate, my front on the T-shirt he'd laid out. I heard the *clink* of his belt, the sound of his zipper going down, then he was behind me. He spread my legs wider, resting his heavy cock against my swollen lips, but not pushing inside.

He leaned over my back, mouth to my ear. "I liked you showing me what to do, darlin', what you like. I love to please you, give you what you need. But you want more, more from me, don't you, sweetheart? You want this?"

I sobbed, so desperate for him I hurt. "Yes."

"Taking care of you makes me so goddamn hard." He nipped my ear, forehead pressing into my shoulder. "But, Abigail, I think I need this, too...to hold you down, to tell you what I want and how I'm going to give it to you. I think you feel it as well, don't you? You're so wet, angel. You love it when I take control."

"Yes," I cried out.

He shoved his cock inside me without warning, and I screamed, coming instantly, too far gone to last another second. Eli grunted and slammed into me from behind, powering his massive dick in and out of my spasming, clenching walls, grunting and growling. I instantly felt another climax start to build; the exquisite ache I got from his cock stretching me, hitting me deep, had me close to the edge fast. He grew thicker inside me, and I grabbed at the cold steel under my hands, desperate for purchase. I found none.

But he pulled out suddenly, before I got there again. I moaned in frustration, then for another reason when his fingers slid through my sensitive lips, up to my ass. He slicked them over my clenching hole as he pushed his cock back inside me, all the while he teased my ass with his finger.

"Abi?" he gritted.

I moaned, knew what he was asking me. "Yes. Do it." I wanted to be so full of him I couldn't think straight. I wanted him to take from me whatever he needed.

He started to shake, a deep groan rumbling from him as he eased his finger in my ass. I pushed back, wanting more, the sensation of fullness foreign but so damn good.

"All right?" Eli rasped.

"So good."

His other hand, resting on my hip, disappeared. "Hands above your head." I did as he asked, and he wrapped his fingers around both my wrists and pinned them to the bed of the truck—then he pushed that finger deeper and at the same time snapped his hips forward.

I cried out, so full all I could do was writhe and moan. I wanted to push back, but Eli was now in full control. He started fucking me again, that finger in my ass, not moving, just planted deep while he slammed his cock in and out of me. I lost all control of my body. My muscles trembled, sweat coating my skin, noises coming out of me that I'd never made in my life. Eli was fucking me so hard my feet were off the ground.

I knew what I wanted and Eli did, too, because he hissed, then grunted, rasping in my ear. "God, I want to punish that tight ass with my cock, Abigail."

"Do it," I gasped.

He released me, pulled his cock and finger free, and flipped me onto my back, looming over me. "Eyes on me."

Then his finger was back, sliding over my ass. I was so wet, there was no resistance when he breached the tight ring of muscle again. I gasped and arched, reaching down to rub my clit, because I *had* to. Pleasure overwhelming me, making me sob and cry out. He pushed in deeper, and my mouth opened on a low groan.

Eli was shaking so hard the truck was shaking with him. "Look at me, darlin'."

I forced my eyes open.

"I want it so bad. I want to claim every part of you, angel."

"Y-yes."

He rammed his cock back inside me. "But we're both gonna have to wait. I don't want to hurt you. I need to make sure when we do it, we do it right."

I sobbed again, and he slid out, then back in, jaw tight, eyes laser focused on me, lighting me on fire, and I lost it completely, crying out, begging, clawing at his shoulders while I rubbed my clit faster.

He shook his head, making a rough sound. "Keep your hands up. It's my job to make you come."

Clamping the fingers of one hand back around my wrists, he pinned them above my head again. He pulled his finger from my ass, then slid his arm under my lower back, lifting me so I had no choice but to wrap my legs around his waist. Then holding me completely immobile, he fucked me stupid. Jarring, brutal thrusts that made it almost impossible to draw breath.

I screamed, coming again, inner muscles clamping down on his cock.

Elijah cursed and slammed in so deep, I knew I'd feel him for days.

"Jesus Christ." He released my wrists, cupped my face, and kissed me, tongue tangling with mine. And God, his deep groans as he came shook me to my foundation. His cock pulsed as he filled me, pumping me full of him.

He finally slowed his thrusts, gliding in and out of me, his body trembling. "That's my good girl," he murmured, lips brushing mine, voice softer than I'd ever heard it. "That's my beautiful girl."

His praise warmed me in a way I didn't understand, but right then didn't have the energy to think about, either. None of this made sense, these intense feelings I had for him, but it felt right, and that's all I cared about. When he finished, he carefully pulled out and rested his forehead against mine. "Darlin'?" he whispered. "Darlin', tell me you're okay."

I cupped his face and gently kissed him. "I'm more than okay," I whispered back.

He stood and toed off his boots, then after he'd shucked off his jeans, he lifted me, cradling me in his arms, and headed toward the lake. He walked straight out into the water and sank down to our chests. It was cool and welcoming against my overheated skin.

He kissed me again, still murmuring sweet things, making me feel like the most treasured woman in the world. His lips pressed against my forehead as his hand dropped between my thighs, sliding over me with a gentle touch, cleaning me under the water, making me sigh with pleasure.

"You sure you're okay?"

I slid my hand around the side of his muscular throat and held his gaze, the worry there making my chest hurt. "That was the single best experience of my life, Eli Hays." I wrapped my arms around his neck. "I don't know what this is, but I know I want it with you, only with you." I kissed his gorgeous mouth. "Don't second-guess yourself." My cheeks heated, which was ridiculous after all we'd done, but I'd never said this out loud, this feeling inside me. "I want what you gave me, Elijah. I loved it when you held me down and told me what to do…and I loved it when I pleased you and you praised me for it. I don't know what it means. I just know I crave it from you, all of it." I swallowed, licking my dry lips. "And I…I think you feel that way, too?"

He stared at me, his breathing rough, his hold getting tighter. "I feel that way, too," he said so low and deep that his words vibrated through my chest.

Relief flooded me, not that I really had any doubt, but I didn't know if he'd ever admit to that part of himself, at least not when he wasn't inside me. "Trust your instincts," I said softly. "That's all you have to do."

His hand slid into my hair, fingers fisting gently, and he kissed me until we were both breathless, until he was hard again. He maneuvered my body so I was straddling his hips, and he slid back into me under the water.

I clung to his wide shoulders, while he followed his instincts—and made love to me in the lake.

• • •

I sipped my iced tea, holding Eli's in my other hand, and headed out of the house. This last week had been one of the best in my life. It had just been me and Eli, well, except for a short visit from James on his way out of town. Eli had stayed in the field working, but to put his mind at rest, I'd sat on the porch with my friend to have our beer. We'd chatted, and everything was like it always was between us, like he'd never left Deep River. But I'd known Eli was watching us from under the brim of that cap—and though it was wrong, and I sure as heck didn't want him to be jealous or insecure, knowing his eyes were on me the whole time had excited the hell out of me. He'd told me that morning, when he knew James was coming out, he didn't mistrust me; it was everybody else he mistrusted. He knew his fears were irrational, but he hated the thought of James touching me.

So when my friend pulled me in for a hug, like he always did, I didn't know what to do. I'd had no choice but to give him a quick squeeze back. I'd wanted to. He was my best friend, and that would never change. Eli would have to get used to him and me, and our friendship.

Still, my belly had squirmed as I'd waved good-bye. Butterflies going crazy while I'd stood there, rooted to the spot, Eli striding across the yard toward me. He'd reached me before the dust had settled behind James's car.

He hadn't said a word, just grabbed my hand and dragged me inside, then he'd shoved down my underwear, pushed me up against the wall, and fucked me.

I loved this new side to him, the side that just acted, that didn't weigh every action, every word. It was happening more lately.

I found him around the side of the barn, stacking wood. A tree had fallen in one of the fields, and he'd been chopping it up for firewood. He turned to me when I rounded the corner, and my breath seized in my throat. He was wearing jeans and boots and nothing else, the heavy belt buckle he wore tugging the soft denim down at the front, giving me an enticing view. The way the sexy rail of dark hair below his belly button thickened…

His cock hardened behind his zipper, and my eyes darted up to his. They were a little wild, and a lot hungry.

I plastered an innocent smile on my face. "I brought you

a drink."

He didn't say anything, just walked over, took it from my hand, and chugged the lot. Then he took mine from my hands, set it on the woodpile, and crowded me against the wall. "You can't look at me like that while I'm working."

I blinked up at him. "Like what?"

His lips tugged up on one side, and my heart fluttered in my chest. He'd been doing that a lot lately as well. Grins, soft smiles, when he looked at me. I'd made it my mission to make him do it as often as possible.

He slid a hand up my thigh, under my dress. "You know what."

I sucked in a breath as his hand drifted higher. "Enlighten me."

He cupped me over my panties, sliding a finger along my slit. "Like you want to drop to your knees and suck me," he said in that gritty voice.

I was flat-out panting now. "And how is that a problem?"

His eyes drifted shut for a few seconds. He licked his lips. "Darlin'," he groaned. "I've got work to do, and you're a goddamn distraction." He nipped my lower lip, then sucked it gently.

"I am?" I gripped his belt buckle; my other hand slid down to his ass and squeezed. "I had no idea."

"You're wearing this pretty dress in front of me, knowing I wouldn't be able to resist putting my hand up under it." His finger continued to torment me, and I clung to his biceps so my weak knees didn't give out. "Before..." His breath came out on a shudder. "When I'd only ever dreamed of touching you like this, when we'd take our trips to town...I used to make sure I was there waiting when you walked out the door, just so I could see which one you were wearing, watch the way it would cling to your thighs when you walked toward me, the way it cupped you right here..." He cupped between my thighs more firmly. "I lived for it, angel. Heaven and hell, every damn time I saw you. I think…" His gaze sharpened, and he licked his lips, watching me in an intense way, making sure he didn't miss my reaction to his next words. "I think you need to be punished for tempting me like this, teasing me when you know I can't do anything about it until tonight."

He was still a little wary about this new dynamic between us, worried that he could hurt me or that he might be too rough. I did my best to prove otherwise every chance I got. God only knew why I was doing this right now, when I knew damn well we were expecting a possible new client at any moment. The guy owned a large ranch a couple of hours from here. He'd heard good things about our horses and the way Eli trained them and was looking to buy at least four. It was a big deal, and we both knew it.

But I was wet and achy, and at the mention of punishment, had to snap my thighs together. I couldn't stop myself from pushing a little more. Dropping my forehead against his chest, I kissed and sucked his bare skin. "What kind of punishment?"

"Abigail." He gritted his teeth. "I should turn you around, press you into that wall, and fuck the hell out of you for testing me like this." A second later, I *was* spun around, facing the steel wall of the barn, and Eli had tugged up my dress. He slammed into me, tugging down my underwear, grinding against me. His lips brushed my ear. "Instead, I'm going to give you a little taste of what you're getting tonight for teasing me like this." His weight disappeared, and the sun only had a second to heat the bare skin of my ass before his hand came down on my right cheek.

I cried out in shock. It stung for a second, but then my skin heated deliciously. I drew in a breath to say something, anything, when he did it again, and this time I moaned. "Holy shit."

He smoothed that hot, rough hand over my throbbing ass.

Then his mouth was at my ear again. "I'm going to spank this ass, then I'm going to fuck it. You think about that all day, Abigail, what's going to happen when our meeting is over and we're all alone." Then he pulled up my panties, dropped my dress, and turned me around.

He was still crowding me. I was struggling to breathe through the out-of-control beating of my heart, the pulsing, throbbing beat between my thighs, deep inside me, when he cupped my face and bent down, pressing his lips to mine, and kissed me hard and deep.

"What the fuck?" someone shouted.

Eli pulled away, and I spun toward the voice, wincing when I saw Kyle standing there.

Oh shit.

Our secret would be all over town before the end of the day.

Chapter Ten

"Why is he touching you?" Kyle shouted.

Eli stepped away from me, turning toward him, hard, scary eyes locking on the smaller man.

I stepped forward, in front of Elijah. "What are you doing here, Kyle?"

"I came to see you." His lips curled. "But instead I find you with this fucking wack job."

"Don't say one more damn word…"

"Why?" Kyle snarled. "Because you know it's true, Abi?"

"No…"

He flung an arm out, motioning to us. "That's the most disgusting thing I've ever seen. Jesus Christ. Have you fucked that monster? Did you let him put his filthy dick in you?"

I jerked like he'd struck me, anger firing through my veins. "We're not doing anything wrong," I yelled back.

"No? Are you serious? Have you lost your mind? He's a murderer, Abi. He killed someone!"

I shook my head, the denial coming out of my mouth before I knew what I was doing. "It's not true. None of it."

"Of course it is!" Eli's boots scraped as he took a step forward.

I stepped back at the same time, trying to use my body to hold Elijah back. "You're the only disgusting monster I can see, Kyle Harris. Now get the hell off my ranch."

"I can't believe you turned me down for that," he yelled. "For that…thing."

"Leave!"

"Someone needs to say something. That monster is liable to murder you in your bed, take a kitchen knife to you like he did his old man."

I was shaking my head, trembling I was so angry. "You don't know him. How dare you come to my place and insult him like that."

"Wait till I tell everyone you're this psycho's whore…"

Eli lifted me bodily when that ugly word flew from Kyle's lips. He placed me out of his path and headed toward Kyle. Kyle's eyes went wide, and he started backing up.

"Don't you ever talk about her like that," Elijah said in a low, terrifying voice. "Ever."

Before Eli could reach him, Kyle spun and ran to his truck. He tore off down the road a few seconds later.

I stood there, fists clenched at my sides, pulse racing, angrier than I could ever remember being. Dread fired through me. "He's going to head into town and run his mouth off to anyone who will listen."

Eli was still staring at the road, back wide and rigid, so still, he looked like a statue. When Kyle's truck disappeared around the bend, he turned to me.

"Eli…"

"That bothers you?"

I stared back. "What?"

"That Kyle will talk about what he saw here?"

I shook my head. "I don't want them talking about you

like that."

"Is that why you said it was a lie, what I did? Why you said we're not doing anything wrong?" His body was still stiff. "Who are you trying to convince, Abigail? Him or you?"

"No, that's not it." I hugged myself tighter, swallowing the lump forming in my throat. "No...the things he was saying about you...I didn't want them talking about you like that, I didn't want..."

"I don't care what they say about me." He moved in, stopping right in front of me. "I don't care what Kyle fucking Harris thinks about me. It's only your opinion that matters." He crossed his arms. "Why were you standing in front of me?"

I blinked up at him. "I...well, I didn't want..." I trailed off, not sure how to answer.

"Did you think I'd hurt him?"

"No!"

"So you think I need you to protect me, that I need you to fight my battles, that I'm too weak or brainless to defend myself against a man like that?"

"No." I shook my head and stepped closer. "Of course not."

He stepped back, denying me, not letting me touch him. It was the worst kind of punishment he could ever dish out.

"I may not talk much to the folks in town, but that's because they're not worth the energy. *He* isn't worth the energy. I'm not simple or slow...or goddamn pathetic."

"I know that..."

"I may not have fucked a woman before you, darlin', but that doesn't mean I'm not a man. It doesn't mean I'm not capable of looking after you the way you need to be looked after." He planted his hands on his hips, letting out a rough breath. "I sure as fuck don't need to stand behind my woman when things get ugly."

My mouth dropped open. "Eli..."

"There was no reason for you to try to justify to that asshole what we were doing." His eyes locked on mine. "Don't you trust me?"

"Of course I do."

I tried to step forward again, but he stopped me with a look. Then, shaking his head, he turned and walked away.

"Elijah, please."

He stopped a short distance from me but didn't look back. "I need to cool down."

How the hell had I messed this up so badly? "I don't think of you like that. God, Elijah…you're the strongest man I've ever met."

He stayed rooted to the spot for several long seconds, then strode away.

I wanted to go after him, make him understand, but I wouldn't be able to, not yet anyway. A truck was heading our way, dust flying out behind it. Our possible new client. This guy could help save the ranch if he liked what he saw, if he wanted to make a deal.

I just hoped I could get through it without falling apart.

· · ·

"I'm looking forward to doing business with you both."

Mr. Lawrence shook my hand, then Eli's, clapping him on the shoulder.

I smiled at the older man. "You won't be disappointed."

This was good news, the best; he wanted our horses, but I was struggling to find any excitement with Eli still not looking at me.

We walked Mr. Lawrence to his truck. Eli stood close, towering over me. I could feel the heat of his skin radiating from him. I wanted to lean into him desperately, but with the sharp line of his spine, the stiff way he held his shoulders, I knew he was still angry.

I waved to Mr. Lawrence as his truck headed out.

Nerves kicked up in my belly as I dropped my hand and turned to Elijah, but he was already walking away. The nerves turned to nausea. Was he going to take off on his horse again? Did he need another night away from me? God, that stung… so damn much.

Had I ruined everything?

I'd hurt him, and I had no idea how to fix it.

I forced myself to go inside, not sure what else to do, what I could say to him to make this better. If he'd even be willing to listen to me if I tried.

The phone in the kitchen was ringing when I walked in, but it stopped before I reached it. *Crap.*

Grabbing a glass, I filled it with water and downed the entire thing. My mouth was dry, like I'd been talking nonstop for the last hour, and more than likely I had. But the new buyer liked our horses, and the money we'd make would allow us to keep the ranch afloat. I stared out the window, watching the dry grass sway with the breeze. Eli's reaction to my defending him was eating at me, mainly because there was some truth to what he said. Not the part about him being a lesser man, and I'd never doubted his intelligence. But the part about Kyle not being worth it? He was right. I'd tried to justify our relationship to that creep. Denying Eli's past, when I'd never cared if it was true or not, trying to convince Kyle, someone who meant nothing to me, that what we were doing wasn't wrong? It was as good as admitting to Eli that I felt the opposite.

Shit.

I rubbed my aching eyes and paced the kitchen. I'd let the gossips and busybodies get to me. I hadn't even realized I'd bought into their crap until those words had tumbled out of my mouth. Not everyone in Deep River was like that. But it was the people with nothing better to do than pass judgment and look down on others who tended to have the loudest voices.

The phone rang again, and I snatched it up. Cassie's shrill voice blasted my ear. I had no idea what she was saying, but I knew exactly why she was calling. Kyle hadn't wasted any time. It'd only been a few hours.

"…what do you think you're doing with that man?" she finished.

I was already angry over what Kyle said, over my own reaction to his words—that I'd managed to hurt Eli. I didn't need this. Definitely not right then. "I love you, you know I do, Cass. But how is it any of your damn business?"

That shut her up, but only for a few seconds. "We love you, too. We've known you since you were a little girl. That's how it's our business."

I shoved my fingers in my hair, pushing it away from my face. "Then you know I'm not stupid or reckless. You're making assumptions, about me and about Elijah…and you know what, I don't need to explain my actions to you or any damn person in this town. He's a good man, he makes me feel special…that's all you should be worried about. I'm happy, Cassie. That should be enough for you."

She sighed. "If that's true, honey, then why did you keep this a secret from me?"

I had my reasons, reasons I believed were good ones. Now, though, they didn't seem good. They seemed like I was ashamed of Eli, of what we were doing, and that wasn't how I felt. God, I'd messed this whole thing up completely. "That was a mistake," I said quietly. "Our relationship is not a secret, it's just new. I just…"

Eli walked in then. He didn't stand there and wait. He walked right up to me, crowding me, surrounding me with his scent, his warmth. Cassie had started on her rant again, and I didn't hear a word; all I could focus on was the man in front of me, the determined expression on his face.

"Say good-bye," he said quietly.

"Cassie? I have to go."

"We're not done talking about this."

"I am. I'll call you in a couple days."

"Abi…"

"Good-bye." I ended the call and looked up at him, desperate to touch him but not sure if he wanted me to. An ache began in the center of my chest. "Are you still mad?" I whispered.

He shook his head, took my hand, and led me outside. He carried on across the dry, scorched earth that was my yard and toward the barn. Our horses were saddled and standing out front. We stopped beside them, and I stroked Bess, saying hello to my horse, then looked at Eli and waited for him to tell me what was going on. He didn't say a damn thing. Instead, he wrapped his fingers around my waist and plonked me in my saddle, passed me my hat, then climbed onto Gus and headed out.

Elijah was a man of few words; I knew this, and I was getting used to our conversations. When he spoke it was because whatever he wanted to say was important to him, so I listened. But his silences could be equally telling. Right now, I didn't think he knew what to say, how to express the way he was feeling. He was going to show me. He was also asking me to trust him.

And I did. Every part of me trusted every part of him.

So I followed. I didn't need to know where we were going. Elijah would take care of me, protect me, make sure I had everything I needed. I realized in that moment that I'd follow him anywhere. That thought should have freaked me out. It didn't.

We rode for a long time, maybe a couple of hours, and

we were nearly to our destination when I realized where he was taking me. The old trapper's hut came into view a few minutes later. It had been here since before my grandfather owned this ranch. I used to come here with my dad sometimes when I was a kid. He and the ranch hands would use the place to sleep or cook when they were working on this side of the property. The ranch was big and not all of it could be used for grazing. Some of it was wild and untamed. The hut was in our farthest field, where the pasture ended and nature took over.

I always thought it was so beautiful, but I hadn't been out here in years.

Elijah dismounted, walked over to me, lifted me off Bess, then led her and Gus away. I stood there watching as he removed their gear, went to the small shed by the cottage, and came back with some hay.

Leaving them to graze, he returned to me and held out his hand. I took it without question. I could tell this pleased him.

When he pushed open the cabin door, my jaw dropped. The rough-sawed walls were cobweb-free, and there was a large striped mat on the floor. The old couch had a gray woolen blanket over it, and the two small steel-framed cots that had always been there had been replaced with a full-size bed. The frame was rustic and chunky, and I could smell new linen and wildflowers. My mouth went dry. "Did you make the bed?"

"Yes."

My heart fluttered, squeezed. The quilt covering it was yellow, my favorite color, with a delicate floral print, frills around the edge, similar to my own. "And the quilt…"

"I know you like flowers."

There was a chipped crystal vase there as well, filled with straggly wildflowers, looking a little worse for wear. I swallowed the lump in my throat. God, to me they were the most beautiful flowers in the world.

He was standing behind me now. I turned to him, and he was studying me, a flush of color darkening his cheeks.

I pulled off my hat and flung it on the couch. "This is where you come? Those nights that you're away?"

He dipped his chin. "Sometimes."

"When did you do all this?"

"Last time I came out." He was looking at me from under his thick lashes. "Wanted to bring you out here…have for a long time." His eyes turned midnight. Fathomless pools that went deep, so damn deep. "Thought a lot about what it'd be like to bring you here. Ever since the day I first saw it after I showed up at the ranch and your father took a chance on me, gave me a job."

My limbs were suddenly weak, his words, everything he'd done to this place, hitting me square in the chest.

"I got out of my truck that afternoon, and the first thing I saw was you. You were on your horse, coming in, skin glistening, golden hair shining in the sun. I'd always thought you were the most beautiful girl I'd ever seen, but that day, I looked at you and my mouth went dry. My heart pounded in my chest. It was like I was seeing you for the first time." He took a step closer. "I went back to the grubby little shack I'd been calling home and stroked my cock with your face in my head, imagining it was your hands on me. You're the only face I see anymore, Abigail. The only woman I've ever wanted."

"Eli…"

"What you said to Kyle today, it scared me, darlin.' I just got you, and I'm afraid you're going to let them tear us apart."

My heart was pounding in my chest as well. He didn't need to say who "they" were. I knew exactly who he meant. The people in this town who weren't happy unless they were sticking their noses in other people's business.

"I won't let them tear us apart. I won't." How had we gotten to this place, come this far? How was it that I craved this man, his touch, more than cool water on a scorching-hot day?

The way he was looking at me, like he was waiting for me to move just so he could pounce, had me heating up, squirming, excited. "Why did you bring me here? What did you want to show me?"

"When I come out here, I allow myself to go there in my head, that place I always thought was bad. I allow myself to think about all the things I thought were wrong or sick and twisted." His nostrils flared. "I used to imagine us here on a winter's night, snowed in. Just us and a bed. What I'd do to you, the way you'd look, the way the firelight would make your bare, sweat-slicked skin glisten." He took another step closer. "How you'd look on that bed while I held you down, made you beg. The way you'd strain under me…" He dragged in a rough breath. "I didn't want to show you anything, Abigail. But I do want to do things to you. Does that scare you?" He took the last step, and we were so close my chest brushed his abs. "Or does it make you wet, like I used to imagine it would?"

"It…" I had to clear my throat; it was too tight to speak. "It…makes me wet." I lifted my chin, looking up at his strong features, the way he watched me, the way the muscle in his jaw jumped, the way every muscle bulged and strained, his control barely leashed. "God, Elijah. It makes me so wet."

His chest expanded, breath releasing on a deep rumble. "You earned a punishment today, didn't you, darlin'?"

My knees started to shake. "Yes."

"What did I say you'd get for teasin' me?"

The ghost of that slap to my behind still lingered. There was no pain, but I'd been aware of it all day. "You said you'd spank my ass for making your cock hard when you couldn't do anything about it."

"And what else?" He said it so deep, it set off a little

quiver that traveled all the way down to my toes.

"Then you'd…you'd fuck it."

He brushed his thumb over the swell of my cheek, down under my bottom lip. "Did you think about that all day, Abigail?"

"Yes." I had. God, I'd been a mixture of worry over what had happened between us and throbbing arousal.

"Have you been hot and aching, imagining what it'll be like?"

"Yes."

He stepped away and walked to the bed, then he took off his shirt and sat down on the edge. "Take off your clothes and come here."

Holy shit. Eli was going to spank me, and I'd never been more turned on. I did as he said. I toed off my boots, then shucked my shorts. His eyes never left me as I dragged my tank top over my head and walked to him.

He spread his solid thighs, hands going to my waist, and drew me closer. "Naked," he said, voice gritty.

I reached behind and undid my bra, belly in knots, thighs slick, nipples tight and hard, aching. I reached down to slide off my panties, but he stopped me. His fingers were hot and dry when he slid them up the backs of my thighs then underneath the fabric to cup my ass. His head dropped forward and he kissed my belly. Then, holding me in place with one hand, he reached down with the other, dragging it up between my legs. He cupped me over my underwear, feeling the proof of my arousal, pressing just for a moment, making me moan.

"Christ, darlin'. Love how wet you get for me." He pushed a foot between mine, making me step out, then brushed his thumb across the top of my thigh.

The pad of his thumb grazed me, his other hand still on my ass, holding me in place, and I whimpered, fighting not to grab his hand and put it where I wanted it.

Finally, he gripped the sides of my panties and slowly slid them down my legs. I stepped from them, and he flung them to the side and sat back. "Shit, look at you. So goddamn beautiful." He slid a single finger through my slick folds, then sucked it between his lips. "Taste so good, darlin'. So good. Can't get enough. Could spend all week buried between your thighs and still not get enough of you." He put his hands on either side of his thighs, tilted his head back, and held my gaze. "Lie over my lap, Abigail. Ass in the air for me."

I was breathing so fast I thought I might hyperventilate. I did as he asked, lying across his lap. His thighs were spread, supporting me, and the denim of his jeans was rough against my nipples.

His hand went straight to my bare ass, smoothing and rubbing, massaging my skin. "So pretty," he rasped. "So damn perfect." He trailed his hand up my spine and down again, his touch tender, reverent. "Why are you getting punished, Abi?"

"I teased you."

His hand squeezed my tender cheek a little harder. "And the other reason, what is it, darlin'?"

Oh God. "I made you feel...I hurt you today...I..."

"No," he growled, cutting me short. "You didn't hurt me, Abi. You didn't trust me. I need your trust more than I need my next breath. I *need* it, Abigail."

I opened my mouth to say he had it, but my words were cut off when his hand came down on my ass.

It barely made contact with my skin.

He'd pulled back.

I wanted what he'd given me this morning. His hand coming down hard on my backside, that deep ache. His thighs trembled, stomach muscles jumping, breath choppy. He was struggling, second-guessing what we were doing, fighting himself.

I lifted my hips, wiggling my ass. "I can take it, Eli."

He cursed.

"Harder, please."

A growl rumbled from deep in his chest, fingers flexing against my cheek, then they were gone. His hand came down again, this time harder.

I cried out.

"Are you going to give me your trust?"

I gasped. "Yes. You have it."

He spanked me again, two in quick succession, but not in the same place, then the heat of his palm was covering my stinging cheek, rubbing and massaging again, making me groan. The sting quickly vanished, replaced with a deep ache that had my thighs shaking and my core clenching.

"Are you going to tease me again?" His voice was tight, deep with hunger.

I squirmed. "If this is what I get…yes," I admitted.

He groaned. "Fuck."

His cock was long and hard beneath me, poking into my belly. That, plus the way he'd said that rough curse, had me aching for more. I spread my legs wider, moaning as I did. Teasing him like I said I would. Pushing him to hit me again. Desperate for it.

Eli stilled, and I knew he was looking at me, at how wet I was. He cursed again, then he spanked me harder. Three times.

I nearly came.

He rubbed and squeezed, deepening the ache, then he did it again. "Spread wider."

I did as he said.

His hand came down between my legs, the wet slap against my swollen lips tipping me over the edge. I screamed and started to come. Eli growled and pressed his hand against my convulsing flesh, applying pressure, rubbing, dragging it out.

Before I could catch my breath, he gently turned me so he could cradle me in his massive arms.

He brushed the hair back from the side of my sweaty face. "Okay, angel?"

I rested my head against his chest, clinging to him. "Yes." That's all I could manage. I was feeling so many different things in that moment, but there was no way I could verbalize a single one.

Eli held me tight, nuzzling me, kissing me. "You did so good, darlin'. So good," he rasped into my hair. "God, you blow me away, sweetheart."

His praise made me happy in a way I'd never experienced, like there was a light shining inside me, bright and warm. I opened my eyes and looked up at him. His expression was soft, lips parted, awe, affection, excitement in his eyes. He was beautiful.

"The way you came like that..." He seemed as lost for words as I was. He leaned in and pressed his lips to mine. "It felt good, didn't it, Abigail? You liked what we just did?"

My ass throbbed in the best way, and I'd just come so hard, my sex was still lightly pulsing. To say I *liked* it was a gross understatement. "Yes. God, Eli, yes. So much."

His rough-skinned hand slid down to my ass, smoothing over a tender cheek. He nuzzled my hair again. "Everything I ever imagined...the way you just came against me like that... shit, angel, you surpassed any fantasy I've ever had."

My nipples pebbled. "Mine, too."

A sound vibrated from his chest, deep and low. "God, Abi." He tilted my face up and stared into my eyes, the muscle in his jaw ticking. "You're all soft and sated in my arms, looking at me that way you do, and all I want to do is protect you, look after you, make you feel good. Will you let me, darlin'?"

"Yes." I touched his cheek. "I want to take care of you, too."

His breath released on a rough exhale, and his hand slid from my ass to between my thighs. He rubbed gently, and I moaned, hips moving with his hand before I knew what I was doing.

"You ready for more?" he rasped. "Because I want inside you so bad it hurts."

"Yes. Please."

His nostrils flared. "Sweetheart, I want to hold you down and fuck you so hard the walls shake." His fingers dipped between my cheeks, and he massaged me there, toying with my ass, sending a shiver of need through me. "Abigail, I want to claim every part of you. Will you let me?"

Chapter Eleven

His body trembled, hungry need in his eyes. He wanted this from me, badly. His hands traveled restlessly over my bare skin. "You like my fingers inside here…" He pressed the tip against my hole, and I bore down on it, or tried to. He held me still. "Don't you, angel?"

I was wet between my thighs, swollen and throbbing. I wanted it. I wanted whatever he wanted to do to me. I don't know what that said about me, but I didn't care. It felt right. All of it. "I love everything you do to me," I whispered. "You make me ache, Eli."

His breath was shaky when he released it. "I'll make it good. I'll make you come so hard."

His cock was a steel rod under me through his jeans, and I wanted it in me in a way that went beyond desperate.

He kissed my lips, then lifted me and placed me on the bed. "Lie back. I'm going to play with you for a while first, get you so damn wet you're begging for it, darlin'. Need to fuck you before I flip you over and slide into your tight ass." He reached down and cupped his cock through the denim, squeezing while his gaze roamed over my skin.

He'd been growing more confident over these last couple of weeks, the things he said, did. But this was something else, new, and hearing those dirty words coming from his lips had me writhing on the bed.

"Hold on to the headboard and don't let go."

I lifted my hands over my head instantly.

His chest expanded with his sharp inhale, his breath coming out rough, shaky. "I did some research on the computer." Color rose in his cheeks. "Wanted to make sure we did this right. I couldn't bear it if I hurt you." He ran a hand through his hair, and his abs tightened.

"Did you like what you saw?" I asked.

His lips parted and his breathing grew heavier, gaze moving over my body stretched out in front of him. "Yes. Lots of things I want to show you, do with you."

An image of Eli's big frame hunched in front of the computer, looking at porn, filled my head, and I swallowed. "Did you...did you get turned on, while you watched?"

He came up beside me and climbed onto the bed, straddling me. "I got so hard, Abi." He leaned forward, rough fingers wrapping around my wrists, still above my head, and pressing them into the mattress. "Imagining it was you being spanked"—he met my eyes—"played with, fucked hard. That it was me using toys on you, making you come so hard you screamed..."

I tried to reach for him, but his hold was too tight. I wanted to touch him so badly, but he was having none of it. Then, before I could beg him to let me, he leaned down and sucked one of my nipples into his mouth, nipped, then sucked again hard. I bucked against him, pulling against his fingers manacling my wrists. He'd scooted lower, and his heavy thighs trapped mine, forcing them shut.

It was torture. I was so hot and desperate, needing him

inside me so bad, I thought I might lose my damn mind.

"I had to shove my boxers down and stroke my cock," he murmured against my damp flesh.

The image bombarded my mind and I shuddered, squirmed against him, needing more contact, desperate for his weight, his cock pounding inside me. But he kept me trapped, sucking and nipping me until my nipples were hard and swollen and I was soaking the bedcovers under me.

He shifted down my body. "I'm going to release your hands, but you have to keep them where they are, understand?"

"Yes."

He began his slow descent, sucking and kissing his way down my body, finally allowing me to spread my legs. I groaned when the cool air hit my overheated flesh. "Put your mouth on me. Please, Eli."

He pressed his palms against my inner thighs, eyes locked between my legs, and groaned. "Oh shit, angel. Look at you. Look how gorgeous you are." He licked his lips. "Goddammit, sweetheart." He slid his fingers over my inner thigh, a little higher but not high enough, touching the proof of my arousal. "I did this to you." He groaned again. "How the hell did I get so damn lucky?"

I was panting now, close to crying I was so desperate for him. His words had me gripping at the wooden slats above my head. I wanted to touch myself, to relieve the ache.

On a ragged moan, he lowered himself to the mattress and pressed his lips to my slick core. He moaned again, then opened his mouth over me, swiping his tongue through my center. I cried out and tried to lift my hips for more, but he held me down, held me where he wanted me, and took his time licking and sucking and nipping until I was a babbling mess begging for his fingers, his cock. Begging him to let me come.

Tears were running down my face when he finally shoved

two thick fingers inside me, wrapped his lips around my clit, and sucked. I screamed so loud my ears rang. My body convulsed, and I ground against him as best I could. He continued to lick and suck me, to fuck me with his fingers. I was trembling, so sensitive I wanted more and to pull away at the same time.

Finally, he climbed from the bed and toed off his boots, then shoved his boxers and jeans down his legs. When he straightened, his cock slapped against his tight stomach, so damn hard and long and thick.

I spread my legs wide. "Yes…yes…" was all I could get out.

He didn't mess around. He dropped on top of me, the hair on his chest rasping over my tender nipples. Then, sliding one hand under my ass, he lifted me and rammed his giant cock deep inside me. I cried out. I hadn't recovered from my last orgasm, and the sudden intrusion, the way that fat head pushed inside me, sliding against that spot, he kicked off another one.

He growled in my ear. "Jesus Christ. Such a hungry pussy." He slammed up into me over and over, sweating and shaking, cursing, fucking me through it. "Can't wait anymore, angel. I was going to drag this out, but now I can't." He pulled out and spun me onto my stomach. "You almost made me come, clutching at me like that. The only place I'm coming tonight is in your ass."

He hauled my hips high, hands skimming down to my cheeks, spreading them, then his mouth was there, licking and sucking my hole. He growled, fingers digging in as he ate at me, that maddening tongue pushing against my quivering flesh.

"Oh, God…Eli. Shit." I fisted the sheets, pushing back.

He tormented me for a long time, until I was desperate for it, for more. Finally, he nipped my ass cheek, then lifted up, reaching for something on the upturned crate by the bed. Lube. The lube I'd had in my bedside drawer. I watched him over my shoulder, watched him squirt some into his hand, then he was slicking it against my tight hole. Anticipation thrummed through me as I watched him rub more on his iron-hard cock. He threw the bottle on the bed beside us, one hand going to my lower back, the other between my legs. "Just relax, Abi. I'm going to take care of you."

The tip of one finger pushed inside, and I moaned.

"That's it, sweetheart, nice and relaxed. Feel good?"

"Yes." I moaned again and pushed back. He slid deeper, doing some groaning of his own. Working that finger in and out of me until I was gasping and trembling. Then, when I was used to it and begging for more, he added a second, stretching me further, preparing me for his cock.

"You're doing so good, angel. So good."

I whimpered.

Finally, he moved up behind me. He leaned forward and kissed my shoulder. "Ready, sweetheart?"

I nodded, grinding back against him.

He slowly pulled out his fingers, then the head of his cock was there, pressing against my ass. I kept watching him, the way his body was bowed tight, the way he gritted his teeth. He pushed some more, breaching the tight ring of muscle, and I gasped. My arms collapsed from under me, my chest dropping to the mattress, and I fisted the pillows.

His hiss was loud. "Okay?" he asked, voice rough as hell. "Am I hurting you?"

"N-no. Keep going."

He rubbed my back, talking softly the whole time, praising me, gentling me as he slid in a little more. He withdrew some, only to come back. He did that little by little, inch by inch, over and over, until he finally slid in all the way. I was so full, stretched so wide, all I could do was pant through it.

"Jesus Christ. So hot and tight." He continued to smooth that wide, rough palm over my back.

I could only nod.

He slid out and then pushed back in, and we both groaned.

"Shit, sweetheart, I need to go faster."

I was lost between pleasure and pain. The feeling confused me, aroused me, had my mind scrambling. My body made the decision for me, and I humped back against him, telling him to do it.

"Oh fuck, angel." Then he started fucking my ass, deep and fast. "Play with your clit, darlin'."

I did what he said, reached down and rubbed at my stiff, slick nub. I didn't think it was possible after already coming so much, so hard, but another orgasm began building almost instantly.

"That's my girl. Make it feel good."

"Please," I groaned. But I wasn't sure what I was begging for.

"I'm gonna come, angel, gonna fill your sexy, tight ass."

His words came out a snarl, deep and distorted with lust. It tipped me over the edge. I screamed, biting the pillow, my ass squeezing down on his cock.

He barked out a curse, heavy thighs trembling against mine, then he pulsed deep inside me and started coming as well. Hot come pumping into me with each erratic thrust of his hips.

When he was done, he carefully pulled out and collapsed against my back, taking me to the mattress on our sides.

One arm was wrapped around me, while the other brushed my hair back. He peppered my neck and the side of my face with kisses. "You did so good, angel, so good." He squeezed me tighter, and the bed shook with the tremors racking his massive frame as he held me. "That's my girl," he rasped. "That's my beautiful girl."

He continued to hold me like that, smoothing his hands over me, kissing me. I could barely hold my eyes open, warmth spreading through me as I lay in his arms. I'd never felt more content or cherished—this connected to another person.

I fell asleep to the sound of his voice telling me I was his.

• • •

After dragging a brush through my hair, I headed outside to find Eli. Four days had passed since he took me to the trapper's cabin, and we'd been living in our own little world since. I'd mostly ignored the phone and its constant ringing. Cassie had given up on trying to "talk sense" into me. Other than a visit from Garrett—and though he hadn't said it out loud, he made it clear he was there to make sure I was still in one piece—we hadn't seen anyone. They truly thought Elijah was capable of hurting me. As soon as Garrett had driven off, I'd flown into a rant. Eli had calmed me down. He always knew how to make me feel better. I'd come to rely on his calming presence. He just made everything right. We felt right together. I was never unsure around him. I knew that he cared about me, would never do or say anything that would cause me pain.

The truck was out front, but I didn't see Eli right away. I headed over to it. We'd sold two horses the day we returned from our overnight getaway. Enough to cover the mortgage for a few months. Things were looking up, and after our meeting the other day, and several more horses going soon, I was actually starting to believe that everything would be okay. There was no way in hell I'd lose this ranch. And now, thanks to Eli's hard work, that wouldn't happen.

"What were you thinking about?"

Elijah's deep voice rumbled behind me, and I spun to face him. He was in his usual jeans and a T-shirt, this time black. His cap was on backward, so I knew he'd been out with the horses. The man was gorgeous, made me tingle all over. Memories of what he'd done to me, what we'd done to each other—dirty promises whispered while he was moving inside me, promises of things to come—filtered through my mind. "I didn't see you there."

His lips tilted up on one side. "I noticed." He moved in close and brushed the backs of his fingers over my cheek. "Why were you blushing?"

I squirmed. My ass cheeks still throbbed from last night. We'd been in the kitchen, Eli at the table while I made dinner. I'd said something about eating less, that I needed to lose a few pounds. He'd tugged me over to him, told me how beautiful I was and to never put myself down like that again. Then he'd thrown me over his knee and spanked me…then fucked me over the table.

When we finally sat down to eat, he'd watched me chew every bite, then took me to bed and made me come with his mouth as a reward. I squirmed again.

"I was…I was thinking about last night."

Heat flashed through his eyes. "You're not the only one." He cupped one of my breasts, the move utterly possessive. He gently squeezed, rubbing his thumb over my instantly hard nipple. "Makes riding a horse damned uncomfortable."

I was already wet, just from that touch alone, ready to jump him if I got half the chance, but instead my mouth dropped open. "Did you just crack a joke, Elijah Hays?"

He grinned wider, flashing his straight white teeth, and my knees nearly gave out. "Looks that way."

"I never thought I'd see the day…"

He grabbed my butt. "You're very sassy for a girl walking around with my handprint on her behind," he said, a wicked glint in his eyes.

I threw my hand up to my chest and faked shock, stumbling back against the truck. "Another one! My heart can't take it."

His chuckle was low and sexy as all hell. "Get in the truck before I throw you over my knee again."

I smirked. "Promise?"

He closed his eyes and sucked in a breath, which is when I noticed his impressive hard-on. "Maybe I'll think of some other way to punish you."

Damn, now I was turned way the heck on and there was no relief in sight. But I was having fun teasing him, so I poked the bear a little more. "Does that mean you've been on the computer again, big guy?"

"Jesus," he rumbled and walked around to open my door. He gave my butt a smack as I climbed in, making me squeak, then walked around and climbed in beside me.

I grinned over at him.

He shook his head.

I poked my tongue out.

His eyes widened.

I burst out laughing.

When I stopped with the giggles, I looked over at him again. He was watching me in a way that made goose bumps lift all over my body. It was warm and hungry, affectionate, and it made my belly swirl with delight.

"Love the way you laugh," he muttered.

"Ditto." I smiled again, and I knew he could see all the things I'd seen in him reflected right back, because he sucked in a sharp breath, murmuring my name before he started the truck and headed down the road toward town.

I hadn't allowed myself to think too hard about what people's reactions would be to us after Kyle had opened his big trap. But it became obvious when we walked in the bank to deposit the check from the horse sale that word had spread among the gossips. Everyone was staring at us like we were the main attraction at a freak show.

Every muscle in my body stiffened, my racing pulse loud in my ears. My skin flushed hot with anger, with betrayal. They were turning on me, on us, and it was an agonizing blow to my heart.

As we were leaving the bank, Mrs. Simms actually had the nerve to shake her head and mutter, "Stupid, reckless, girl." And she wasn't the only one who had something to say.

An unwelcome feeling swirled in my belly, behind my ribs, something alien, its weight growing heavier and heavier with every step we took. I'd seen these people—my people—do this to others…God, to Eli.

I'd never in a million years thought they'd do this to me. I couldn't believe they had the nerve to say things like that, of course not to our faces, just loud enough we'd hear. I'd known most of them all my life. They'd been nothing but friendly and open to me.

Eli was stiff and tense by my side, and the sense of helplessness, the pain I was feeling for him, intensified. I wanted to scream at them on Eli's behalf. I wanted to tell them to leave him alone, not to treat him like this. It was killing me, every minute he was subjected to their scorn. I didn't want that hate directed at him. My natural instinct was to protect him, defend him, not because I thought he was weak or couldn't look after himself but because I felt that way about everyone I cared for. Instead I kept my lips zipped. I knew after the last time, he wouldn't welcome it.

So with my only thought to stop the stares and hateful comments, I moved a little away from him, putting more distance between us. When we walked into Coopers, instead of sitting down to eat, Eli grabbed us a muffin each and coffees to go. He was paying when Joanna, a girl I used to go to high school with and who had worked at the diner ever since, asked, "So it's true, what Kyle said? You two are together?" She motioned between the two of us with the money Eli had given her, eyes bright with excitement. The prospect of getting the details from the horses' mouths too much for her to contain.

I ignored her question and looked up at Eli. "Right, we better get going."

I grabbed the muffins, and her eyes stayed locked on me, like if she looked long enough, I might break and spill all my secrets to her.

"He seemed pretty certain," she said, pushing as she worked out Eli's change and handed it to him.

My palms grew sweaty, the sick feeling in my belly growing more intense. I couldn't take it anymore, their judgment, their looks. The way they were treating Eli like he wasn't a human being. Like they had a right to what was in our hearts, our minds. The way we felt about each other. Just waiting for the chance to dissect something so personal and beautiful and turn it into something sordid. I wasn't going to give them that.

And I just...snapped. "Kyle isn't exactly the most reliable source of information. He was certain about the UFO he saw senior year as well."

She narrowed her eyes, and I spun around and walked out before she could ask any more damn nosy questions.

The drive back to the ranch was quiet. Eli was focused inward, deep in thought, unhappy. My stomach churned. I'd done it again. Spoken without thinking. But I'd been shocked that people, *friends*, people I'd known all my life, could behave that way. Judge us like they had a right, like they knew any damn thing about *us*. I sucked in a breath, closing my eyes when the full impact of what I'd done, of what Eli had faced most of his life, hit me like a ton of bricks.

I started shaking, the ache I felt for him more than physical—it was soul deep. And I'd gone and added to his pain. Again. I thought I might actually vomit. Sick over what I'd said. Over how Eli must feel. Why the hell had I lied? Why hadn't I just admitted what was between us?

I turned to Elijah, my heart in my throat, desperate to make him understand. "I shouldn't have said what I did to Joanna. I'm sorry, Elijah. God, I don't give a shit what an idiot like her thinks, I don't care what any of them think…"

"You did the right thing," he said to the windshield, surprising me. "You were right to deny it." He pulled up to the barn and shut off the engine.

"No." I shook my head. "No, I was wrong. I don't know why I said that… I just wanted them to stop… I—"

He placed his hand tenderly against the side of my face, successfully silencing me. He shook his head. "You weren't wrong." Then he brushed his lips over mine, climbed from the truck, and headed out to the field and the horses.

I watched him go, heart lodged firmly in my throat.

Chapter Twelve

The day was dragging, and the queasy feeling in my belly wasn't showing any signs of subsiding.

The fact that Eli hadn't come in the whole afternoon, had been out working since we returned from town—had been avoiding me—wasn't helping.

I could see him from where I stood at the front of the house, his shirt off, sweat and dirt coating his skin as he mended fences. He'd started the task after he'd run the horses through their paces. Now the sun was dipping low in the sky, and he didn't look like he had any intention of finishing any time soon.

Dinner was almost done. We'd been eating every meal together, and I didn't know if I should leave him to his own thoughts or go out there and try to get him to come in. I hated this, how a pack of ignorant busybodies had managed to get between us, had caused Elijah to doubt what we were doing. Because that's what was happening here. He was torn, conflicted. I'd seen it in his eyes when he'd finally looked at me. When he'd said I was right to deny what was between us.

When Kyle had found us together earlier in the week, he'd said he didn't care what they thought, that they weren't worth the wasted breath. Now, though, after the incident in town…

Well, I didn't know what he was thinking.

I decided to leave him for a little longer, hoping he'd come in when he was ready, and walked back inside. I finished up dinner and left it to cool. We could reheat it later. I didn't want to eat alone. I wanted to eat with Eli. Restless and worried, and desperate for something to keep myself occupied, I headed outside to tackle the pile of wood he had been chopping, and began stacking it against the barn wall.

It was almost as tall as me when I heard the crunch of his boots behind me.

I started to turn, but I didn't get the chance. He collided with my back, yanked the piece of wood out of my hand, flung it aside, and walked me forward to the truck parked a few feet away.

His hand dropped to the front of my shorts. "Need you," he growled against my ear. "Will you let me fuck you right here, angel?"

We were behind the barn; even if someone just showed up, they wouldn't be able to see us. And right then, I wanted him so bad I didn't care. "Yes," I gasped out, dizzy from the sudden onslaught, the way he was now tearing at my shorts to get them open. "Is this my punishment?" I wanted it, needed it, deserved it. The guilt over today was eating me up. I needed release from it.

"No," he rasped. "You did nothing to deserve punishment."

"Eli…"

"Don't," he said, cutting me off, agony in his voice. Then he shoved my shorts and underwear down, and I kicked them free. "I need you, right now. I can't get enough of you, darlin'. You're all I can think about, all day, every day. When I'm inside you, I'm in heaven. And as soon as I pull out, all I'm thinking about is when I can get back in."

I twisted in his arms, and he let me. He lifted me off the ground and planted my bare ass on the hood of his truck. His cock was free a second later. He cupped my bottom in one of his massive hands, while I grabbed for his dick, guiding him in.

He slammed up inside me.

I sank my nails into his wide shoulders, mouth dropping open on a moan at the feeling of fullness. It was impossible to think, to do anything but take all of him however he wanted to give it to me. I clung to him while he slammed into me full force, yanking me forward so I met each one of his brutal thrusts.

He grunted, teeth gritted, jarring my entire body every time he pounded into me. I cried out, scratching at his shoulders and back, wanting more, wanting everything he had.

His eyes blazed bright with something I couldn't name, something that was as beautiful as it was painful to look at. "You're my salvation, Abigail," he said, voice low and guttural, each word punctuated with an almost violent thrust of his hips. "Right here, inside you, I'm redeemed. I'm the man you need. I'm yours and you're *mine*."

His words sliced though me, the enormity of what his life had been like, of the way he saw himself. A sob exploded past my lips, forming a coherent reply an impossibility.

Leaning into me, he grabbed my hands, shoving them above my head, and took me down to my back, pinning me against the hood of his truck. "Who owns this pussy?" He ground into me. "The one my cock was made for, the one that gets wet as soon as I touch you?" he snarled.

The answer flew from my lips. "You do."

"That's right." His mouth slammed down on mine, then he rasped against my lips. "Who owns the mouth I'm kissing, darlin'?"

Another sob burst from me. "You do."

He let go with one hand and dropped it down to my ass again, dipping lower, between my cheeks, teasing my hole. "Who owns this tight ass?"

"Oh God. You do!"

He pushed the tip inside, and I screamed, coming so hard I shook, grinding and moaning as I spasmed around his hard-as-steel cock.

He pulled back suddenly and lifted me off the hood. I wrapped my legs around him instantly, and cock still hard and deep inside me, he strode into the barn. It was quiet, the setting sun filtering through the single window on the rear wall, light catching the dust motes drifting around us like glitter. "I need..." He hissed a breath out through his teeth and shook his head. "I need more, Abi." His voice was gritty, deep. "Will you give it to me?"

I didn't know what "more" meant, but I'd give him anything he wanted. We'd tried a few different things since our time in the trapper's cottage, and I'd loved everything he'd done to me. I trusted him to take care of me, to make whatever we did good. "Y-yes."

He gripped my hips, ground into me one last time, then pulled out, groaning deeply as he did. He'd carried me to the side of the barn, where the roof tilted downward. Eli stood me in front of him, gripped the bottom of my tank, and pulled it over my head.

His jeans were still undone, cock enormous and slick with my arousal, so hard and thick. My mouth went dry. I wanted to drop to my knees, take that beautiful dick into my mouth...

"I want to tie you up, Abi. I want you to hand every bit of control to me. Everything."

I swallowed hard, the sound audible.

"Does that scare you?" he choked out. "Are you afraid?"

I shook my head. It didn't scare me. It turned me the hell on. "No. I trust you."

His big body jolted like he still couldn't believe it, like he still expected me to run scared, to turn on him like everybody else. "Hands," he finally said.

I held them out, and he wrapped my tank around my wrists. Then, grabbing one of the lead ropes from the wall beside us, he tied it around the shirt, using it to protect my wrists. Then lifting my hands, he tied the remaining length over a low beam, so they were suspended above my head.

I couldn't move, and I was naked apart from my bra.

His fierce stare raked over me, body heaving, veins bulging under his tan skin. There was so much behind his brown eyes, I had no hope of deciphering what he was thinking, feeling.

"Spread your legs nice and wide for me." I did as he said and he reached down, wrapped his fingers around his cock, and squeezed. "So beautiful. My beautiful angel," he rasped.

I whimpered, heart pounding at his words, the guttural way he'd said them. I was ready for him again, excited and nervous. He trailed his gaze over my body, and I knew, could see it in his eyes, that he was feeling the same thing I was— afraid that what we had could slip away. Elijah felt the control he held on to crumbling. The world as he knew it was shaking beneath his feet, and he was taking back control the only way he knew how.

With me.

Was he aware that was what he was doing?

He was breathing heavily as he came closer, cock painfully hard, balls drawn up tight. He had all his attention focused on me. He'd stopped stroking himself and then reached down and tucked his cock in his jeans, doing them up. The lines etched into his face told me it caused him physical pain.

What was he doing?

He closed the gap between us and slowly walked around

me, dark eyes moving over me as he did, soft touches brushing my skin, tender kisses to my breasts, my hip, the center of my back. He stopped behind me and brushed my hair over my shoulder, kissing the nape of my neck. "How did I get so lucky?" He kissed me there again. "How could you let me touch you?" His hands came around me and cupped my breasts, squeezing gently. "Let me put my big, rough, dirty hands on your pretty, smooth skin, this sweet little body?" He nuzzled the space between my neck and shoulder. "How did I ever deserve that?"

He shook his head.

"Elijah..."

One of his hands smoothed down my belly, sliding between my slick folds. "I don't, angel. I never did."

I wanted to pull him into my arms and comfort him, show him he was wrong. But he wasn't going to listen to me right then. As far as he was concerned, he wasn't good enough, and nothing I could say would change his mind. He'd made it impossible for me to try, impossible for me to reach for him, comfort him, pleasure him.

He'd let me orgasm a little while ago, but he'd held off.

He'd said I wasn't being punished...

And I realized in that moment — he was punishing himself.

His fingers were relentless. I gasped and moaned, head swimming, caught between the pleasure he was giving me and my need to reassure him. "You do...I..."

"Shhh," he said and circled my clit, making me jerk in his arms.

I love you.

The words were right there, a second from exploding from my lips. I did, I loved him with everything in me, but he wasn't ready to hear it. I doubted he'd believe me if I told him. Not after what happened today. Somehow I'd let him in. He'd found a way past my fears and the pain of losing both my parents and filled that empty place in my heart.

He released a ragged breath and moved around me, so he was in front of me again.

"I'd never kissed a woman before you." His hand went back between my legs, and he pushed a finger inside. I cried out, arching, the ropes pulling against my wrists. "You're the only woman I ever wanted to kiss, the only woman I ever wanted."

I whimpered. "I need to touch you, Elijah."

He ignored me like I hadn't even said a thing and dropped his head to my shoulder, breathing in deep. "Did you ever see me like them, darlin'? A monster…a charity case?"

"No. Never."

He lifted his head. "Jesus, Abigail, I was afraid to let myself believe it…but I'm starting to. You see me differently, don't you? You really do care?"

"Yes…"

He cursed, thrust his fingers in my hair, and brought his mouth down on mine, cutting me off. He slanted his head, tongue licking deep, kissing me in a way that had my head spinning. He moaned against my lips as he finger-fucked me. Just that one finger. Making me desperate for more, keeping me teetering on the edge.

"You can't hide the way you feel about me, can you? You love the way my mouth feels on yours."

"Yes, I love it."

"You get wetter when I kiss you, touch you."

He made an anguished sound that sent a shiver down my spine. The way he was looking at me, eyes blazing, teeth gritted, that pain back in his eyes, it was like he'd only just now allowed himself to believe it, believed that I wanted him as much as he did me. After everything we'd done and said, how could he have doubted it?

He shuddered and dropped to his knees in front of me. "I

need to taste you, feel you quivering against my tongue, angel. Lift your foot."

I didn't have a chance to do as he asked because he did it for me, lifting my leg so it rested over his shoulder. I was exposed, wide open. He leaned in, hands on my ass, and buried his face between my thighs before I had a chance to say a thing. His mouth opened over me, licking and sucking my slick, sensitive flesh, then he plunged his tongue inside me. I cried out, fully handing over control, like he wanted me to— like I wanted, too.

He growled, fingers flexing against my ass as heavy-lidded brown eyes lifted to mine, locking on while he fucked me with his tongue. I bucked, my skin flushing hotter. A cry burst past my lips, and I wrapped my hands around the rope above, desperate for something to hang on to. I was completely at his mercy.

He needed this from me, and I didn't want it any other way.

My orgasm began to build, but I wanted it with him inside me, I wanted him to come with me. I moaned, whimpered. "Don't make me come, not without you."

His eyes flashed with determination. "Don't worry, you will, darlin'." Then he shifted his mouth to my clit and slipped that finger back inside me and I flew. He didn't let up until I stopped bucking against him.

Finally, he stood.

I watched him from beneath hooded lids. His body seemed bigger somehow, his chest massive, thighs rock solid. His skin was flushed, muscles bulging. He licked his lips and shoved my bra up, exposing my breasts, then he leaned in and sucked one of my nipples deep.

I thrashed against my restraint, positive I was losing my mind. I'd never experienced anything like this. It was intense. I was desperate for more and not sure I could take another second all at the same time.

I needed him. I needed him inside me. Now. "Fuck me. Fuck me, Elijah. Please."

He made a tortured sound and released my nipple. His expression was pained, and he reached down, hissing as he gripped his cock through the denim and squeezed hard. He shook his head. "Not yet."

His fingers went back between my legs, and I groaned helplessly. I was trembling and sweating now, and just those light brushes over my clit already had me close to coming again. I was dying. I was going to die from lust. I started spasming deep inside. "I can't do it, not again…"

Eli leaned in, sucking my nipple, leaving it nice and wet, then pulled away and slapped it. I wasn't expecting it, and I screamed, slamming my legs together. He gripped my thighs and forced them apart. He hadn't hit me hard enough to hurt, but enough that my nipple throbbed deliciously.

I struggled to breathe. It was like the hard little bud had a direct line to my sex. "Oh God."

He did it again, sucked then slapped, but this time he leaned in and sucked it again after, easing and intensifying the ache at the same time. I tried to slam my thighs shut once more, but this time he was ready and shoved one solid thigh between mine, holding me open.

He repeated the same thing several times, until I was trembling so hard my teeth rattled and my inner thighs were slick. And just when I didn't think I could take another second, Eli touched my clit and I screamed, coming so hard I was seeing stars.

He wrapped his arms around me, holding me through it. Heat washed over me, and I clamped my eyes shut, body convulsing with the pulses deep inside me. Before I was done, I was lifted, hoisted up. My bound hands went over his head, resting behind his neck, my legs wrapping around his waist…

He tore at the front of his jeans, then his cock rammed into me, his mouth coming down on mine. His hands gripped my ass, and he brought me down on his cock over and over again. I clung to him for all I was worth as he fucked me hard and fast in the middle of the barn.

His cock was huge and so hot inside me, then it pulsed and he roared, pumping me full of him. It was too much for my oversensitive flesh, and I bit down on his shoulder as my inner muscles clenched around him, another orgasm flying through me, forcing a broken sob past my lips.

Eli's panted breaths were still brushing my neck as he lifted one hand and undid my restraint. I moaned as blood rushed back to my arms and hands.

He held me close and started walking. I couldn't open my eyes, but I knew he was taking me up to his room.

He laid me down on his bed as soon as we walked in. His hands were gentle, caressing me, stroking me tenderly as he removed my bra, then lay down beside me. The covers came up a second later, and I was instantly wrapped in his arms.

"Rest, angel," he rasped.

"Love you," I mumbled, then passed out.

Chapter Thirteen

I woke to the sound of birds singing, the sun warming my skin, and Elijah's addictive scent surrounding me. Opening my eyes, I twisted to look at the man lying beside me. He wasn't there, though, he was sitting against the headboard, eyes open, one hand behind his head, the other resting on his abs. The sheet was low, draped across his hips, and he was staring up at the ceiling. I reached out, placing my hand on his stomach, running my fingers over the deep ridges, toying with the dark line of hair that disappeared below the sheet.

He tilted his head toward me, hand dropping to mine, stopping my searching fingers from dipping lower.

"Morning," I whispered. His cock was getting harder. I could see it growing with every touch of my fingers.

"Morning," he said softly.

There was something in his voice, in the way he was looking at me, that made me pause. "Did you sleep okay?"

He shook his head.

I climbed to my knees and went to him; his arms dropped away, letting me straddle his hips. "Do you want to talk about it?" If only he'd open up to me, I could work at putting his mind to rest.

His cock was rock hard now. He shook his head again, and my heart sank.

I knew he was bothered by what had happened the day before. I was, too, but it was my life. The people in town didn't get a say in who I had a relationship with. It wasn't up for debate. I just hoped like hell they got bored with us sooner rather than later and moved on to interfering in someone else's life.

Despite the sizable erection poking me in the backside, his lips were held in a grim line. I wanted one of his subtle smiles; better yet, I wanted to hear his heart-stopping laugh. I wasn't going to get that out of him this morning, though. Which meant I had to improve his mood another way.

I lifted up a little and dragged the sheet out of the way. He groaned when my bare sex made contact with his cock. I rubbed up against him, wrapping my arms around his neck, and pressed my lips to his, sucking and licking his gorgeous mouth, working myself up on the fat underside of his dick trapped between us. One of his hands was on my ass, the other sliding up my back to tangle in my hair.

"Let me make you feel good," I said against his lips. I ground down harder, and his mouth opened on a gasp. I took advantage and dragged my tongue over his, tangling and tasting. God, I couldn't get enough of him.

His hand tightened on my butt. "You gonna fuck me, angel?"

"Yes."

He watched me through half-lidded eyes, hand still on my ass, massaging, inviting me to do whatever I wanted, to take what I needed. His cock stood up between us, thick and veined and so damn hard. I reached down, fisted him, lifted up, and sank down, taking him all the way.

"*Oh God.*" I didn't know if I'd ever get used to his size. "So good."

"My beautiful girl's always so wet for me." He wrapped his arms around me, his hold light, giving me the freedom to move how I liked but in a way he'd feel every arch of my spine, every twitch, every roll of my body.

I threaded my fingers in his hair and began to move. "Because I always want you."

His hand tightened in my hair, and he pulled me down, kissing me hard and deep, groaning into my mouth as I fucked down onto him. His hand gripped my butt harder, then he was lifting me, bringing me back down, the pace slow and steady. I could feel all of him, the way he filled me on the way in, dragging out, making me desperate to have him inside me again instantly. "You're so big." I moaned. "Christ, Eli, you go so deep."

He kept on kissing me, tilting his head, fucking my mouth the way he was fucking me—slow and deep.

It didn't take long. I was still sensitive from the night before, and when he brought me down and held me there, grinding up into me, it hit without warning. I pulled back, about to drop my head to his shoulder, but he cupped my jaw with one hand, holding it where he wanted me, making me look at him. Watching my face as I rolled my hips against his, eyes fluttering, mouth open, cries filling the room.

His fingers dug into my hip, and he slammed up into me two more times, then he grunted, pulling my mouth back to his so I could taste his moans, those sexy growls, as he came hard inside me.

I dropped my head to his shoulder, and he smoothed his hands over my back, body sated, sleepy, like I'd been last night. Protected and treasured in his strong arms...

That's when I remembered what I'd said before I went to sleep.

I'd told him I loved him.

I didn't even know if he'd said it back, if he'd even wanted to.

I stiffened, and he tightened his arms around me like he could read my mind.

"Eli…" God, I sounded as unsure as I felt.

"I want to take you somewhere," he said against my hair. "Will you let me show you something?"

"Yes," I said against his skin, heart hammering in my chest. He'd heard me last night; how could he not have? Was that why he was acting strange this morning? Was it more than what happened in town?

My first thought was to wish them back, wish back those two mumbled words said when I was at my most vulnerable, but then I realized I didn't want that. I did love him. I loved him so much, the idea of not having him anymore physically hurt. I didn't know if that was something Eli was ready to hear, but I knew he cared for me. It was in every touch, every long look, every whispered word.

Whatever it was he wanted to show me, it was important to him, and I got the feeling, to us.

I lifted my head. "When do you want to go?"

He smoothed my hair away from my face. "Now."

• • •

Elijah drove us to the other side of town. It was a beautiful day, sun shining but not too hot.

I was sick to death of the damn sun.

We needed rain, badly. Still, I loved this part of the country, couldn't imagine living anywhere else but here. I looked over at Eli. He was deep in thought, that troubled expression back on his face that had been there first thing this morning.

We'd showered together, then he'd taken my hand and led

me to his truck. I had no idea where we were going, and the farther we drove, the more my belly squirmed. Wherever it was made him uneasy. His shoulders were tense, his jaw tight, brows low. Why was he taking me somewhere he so obviously didn't want to go?

My nerves increased, and I ended up just as tense as he was.

Finally he turned down a narrow road lined with cornfields, brown and dry, the drought-ridden earth cracked and lifeless. I pressed my hands between my knees and squeezed them together to stop my hands from fidgeting. At the end of the road was a small house. As we got closer, I could see the paint was chipped, windows broken or gone, the front door left hanging open. The yard was as cracked and dry as the fields around it, obviously abandoned. It gave me the creeps instantly.

Eli pulled up a couple yards away and turned off the engine. His eyes were fixed ahead, locked on that open front door.

I reached out and touched his arm. "Where are we? What is this place?"

He was quiet for several seconds, then finally said, "Home."

He still hadn't looked at me, and I had to work to keep my voice even. "This is where you grew up?"

"Yes." He dropped his hands to his thighs. "I was born in that house, lived there until my mother passed away." He turned to me then. "The day she was buried, I walked out and I never came back."

His pain was thick, a tangible thing. I wanted to reach out, pull him into my arms, but that's not what he needed right then; I could tell by the rigid way he held his body. "Why did you bring me here?"

"I can remember hiding in the cornfields, my mother

screaming for him to quit hurting her... I used to hear them all the time, Abi, those screams. Long after both of them were gone. They'd echo through my mind when I closed my eyes." His eyes drifted shut for a moment, then they were back on me. "You made them go away, angel, you did that... Jesus, you made me feel human again."

"Elijah," I choked out. I tried to scoot across the seat, to get closer to him, but he shook his head. I bit my lip and stayed where I was, but it hurt not to touch him. "Eli, please. What's going on?" Though I thought I already knew, and it was tearing me apart inside.

He held my gaze. There was so much behind his dark eyes, so much anguish, it was hard to keep looking at him. He reached out and brushed his thumb over my cheek. "You can't love me, Abigail."

My breath seized in my chest. "What?"

"This..." He pointed to the rundown cottage that was once his home. "This is where I come from. It's what I am... and it's all they'll ever see." He kept touching my face. "Cassie was right. I'm no good for you. I never was, and I never will be. I'll only fail you...just like I failed my mother."

"No." The word exploded from my mouth, and I shook my head. "You were just a little boy. You didn't fail anyone... and I don't care what they think... I—"

"Everyone in this town loves you. You've suffered enough pain in your life already, losing both your parents. After what you've given me, I can't stand by and watch them make you an outcast as well. Do nothing while they turn their backs on you. I won't."

I reached up, gripped his wrist, and held on tight. "I don't care what any of them think. I don't *care* about any of them..."

"Someone as bright and beautiful as you..." He cleared his throat. "I won't be the reason the sunshine fades in your eyes, sweetheart. I never want you to go through what you did in town again, not because of me. You love people. You love your friends. You'll lose every one of them, all the people you care about, if you're with me. You need to deny it…"

"No!"

"Abi…"

"No," I said again. "You can't tell me not to love you. You can't." My heart ached like it was cracking in my chest. "You mean more to me than all of them put together. I promised. I promised you I wouldn't let them tear us apart, and I meant every word."

He didn't answer, stayed quiet at my side for the longest time. His silence saying more than any words could. We were at an impasse. He wasn't backing down, and neither was I.

Finally, he started the truck and we headed for home.

It took every ounce of strength I had not to fall to pieces. Not to crawl into his lap, wrap myself around him, and never let go. He hadn't said it, but in my gut I knew he was planning to leave Deep River. For me. Because he had some misguided notion that it was for the best, that my life would be better without him. Just the idea of his leaving, of never seeing him again…of not waking up every morning to Eli by my side, shredded me. Broke me. I couldn't…I wouldn't allow it.

I'd told him I loved him, but the man still didn't fully understand what that meant to me.

But he would.

And if I couldn't convince him to stay…

I'd leave it all behind. I'd go with him.

Chapter Fourteen

I stared out the window. A few clouds were dotting the sky, but that bright sun was still there, beating down. I dropped the lace curtain and went to my closet. A storm was gathering, I felt it in my bones. But there was no way it could match the one stirring inside me. Elijah and I had spent the night together, but he was still being quiet, distant, and it was tearing me apart. All evening I'd caught him watching my every move, that silent contemplation, that deep longing in his eyes—those goddamn lips firmly shut. I hated it.

If he thought I'd just let him walk out of my life without a fight, he had another think coming.

I slipped my feet in my yellow flip-flops, straightened my favorite white sundress, then dragged a brush through my hair. I was on a mission this morning, and Elijah was coming along for the ride, whether he wanted to or not.

I strode out of the house toward the truck and, opening the driver's door, flung my bag in. As expected, Eli stopped working on the fence he was repairing a short distance away, dropped his tools, and headed toward me.

I offered up a bright smile as he neared.

He motioned to the truck. "What are you doing?"

"Heading into town." My heart started beating a little faster, but I refused to let him see how nervous I was.

His brow scrunched. "Why?"

"I forgot a few things the other day."

He reached out, hand going to my hip, fingers curling into the fabric, like he could physically stop me from going. I guess he could, if he really wanted to. Well, he could try, anyway.

"What things?" He was frowning now.

Um...crap. I hadn't thought that far. "Women's things," I blurted.

He pulled his T-shirt from the back of his jeans, where he'd tucked it after taking it off, and dragged it over his head. "I'm coming with you."

I knew he wouldn't let me go alone; I'd been counting on it. He was far too protective for that. "You don't have to do that," I fake-protested.

"You're not facing those people on your own."

He led me to the passenger side, and I climbed in. His cap was still on backward, and when he got behind the wheel, I couldn't stop sneaking peeks at him. He was so damn handsome, even when he was frowning, full lips held in an unforgiving line. He was worried for me, and I understood why. Yes, a lot of people cared about me in Deep River. They loved me, and they'd loved my dad. They also knew I didn't suffer fools. Not only were a lot of these people friends, we'd done business together. They knew I had a good head on my shoulders, that I was a decent judge of character. I didn't know what would happen today. Eli and me going to town together could make everything worse, but my theory was the more they saw us together—the more they saw how much he cared for me, how much we cared for each other—the sooner they'd get over it and eventually accept it.

I was doing this for Elijah, not me, and sure as hell not them.

He needed his mind put to rest that I wouldn't lose anyone because of him. At least anyone worth holding on to. I hoped like hell I could show him we could weather this. I just needed one person to act like a civilized human being toward us. Just one.

Tension radiated from him. He was unhappy about this, worried for me. I equally loved and hated it.

We finally reached Deep River, and I pointed to a parking spot in the dead center of town. Market days had everyone crawling out of the woodwork, and it was no different today. The street was busy, lined with stalls, and already a few people had spotted the truck and had stopped to look at us.

He shook his head. "Why don't we park a little farther down the street?"

"Here's fine."

Still frowning, he did as I said, then climbed out, coming around to open my door. He was on guard, in full-on protection mode. He moved in behind me, keeping a little ways back, doing his best to curb talk while trying to act as my own personal bodyguard. I wasn't having any of it. Nope. I ignored my racing pulse, and as soon as we hit the sidewalk, I reached out and grabbed his hand, leaning into his side.

He froze and looked down at me. "What the hell are you doing, Abi?"

I shrugged. "Holding my boyfriend's hand, what does it look like?"

His Adam's apple slid up and down his neck. "Angel," he choked out, "don't do this."

People had stopped to stare, not even trying to hide it. I smiled and waved, greeting people as I usually did. Most mumbled a reply. I held my breath, waiting to see what Eli would do. If he'd pull away and deny us to protect me, or if he'd face these people with me and show them we didn't care what they thought...

He gripped my hand tighter, and I glanced up at him. He held my gaze, his eyes searching, conflicted. For a split second I thought he might pull away, but then he took a step forward—and we started to stroll down the street together, moving deeper into the crowd.

We'd only gone a little ways when Jack Elders, the man who'd bought two horses off us, walked up.

He shook our hands. "Elijah, Abigail, nice to see you both." There was a softness in his eyes when he looked at me, and I had to blink back tears of gratitude. "Thought I'd let you know how well those horses have settled in. You have a magic touch, Elijah Hays. My daughter's taken a shine to the mare. Not sure how much ranch work she'll be doing now that Emily's claimed her."

Eli offered one of his subtle grins. "That doesn't surprise me. She's got a gentle soul. I'm sure she's just as taken with Emily."

Jack's smile widened. "Think you might be right there."

After Jack moved on, things changed, just a little, but they definitely changed. People weren't just staring, they were assessing. There was no way to miss the way Elijah guided me through the crowd, his protectiveness. The way he looked at me, the affection in his eyes. I pulled him to a stop in front of one of the vegetable stalls, making a show of picking out some tomatoes. If people were going to get used to us, they needed to see us together. Eli was uncomfortable, but his shoulders had relaxed a fraction. The Deep River knitting club had a table set up next to the vegetables, and several eyes were now aimed our way.

A chair scraped and Mrs. Chambers, a member of the club, stood and rounded the table, coming right over to us. She was old as dirt and highly respected in the town. She knew everyone, was sweet, quiet, and extremely kindhearted. So when she looked up at Eli and shook her head, I had no idea what to expect, what she might say.

A tight knot coiled in my belly.

"You always were a big boy," she said, grinning when Elijah's eyes widened. "I knew your mama, son, since she was just a girl. She loved you with all her heart."

Elijah stilled beside me. I squeezed his hand.

"She was a good woman, ended up with the wrong man is all." She shook her head and laid her hand on his forearm. "There are a lot of flapping jaws at the moment, but I don't want you to listen to them."

Eli was frozen beside me, and I edged in closer, trying to offer him support. Several people were openly listening now, and with the respect this woman had around here, what she said next could help or hinder my cause.

"You've got none of him in you," she said gently. "None. You've got your mama's eyes and her heart. I've known that since you were a boy. You probably don't remember this, but I used to watch you sometimes. Always so sweet and gentle, kind to others. Glad to see you finally happy, Elijah Hays." Then she walked away, returning to her knitting group.

We both stood there stunned for several seconds. The quiet that had grown around us was slowly being submerged in chatter again. Some people moved on; others continued to stare and whisper.

Still holding Elijah's hand, I led him away from the thickest part of the crowd. When we had some space, I turned to him.

He was still stunned; Mrs. Chambers's words had hit home. Had been exactly what he'd needed to hear.

"See," I whispered. "It's going to be okay." Not everyone in this town would accept him—accept us together. It would take time, more people like Jack and Mrs. Chambers. But that didn't matter, not to me. I'd find out who my true friends were, and the rest…I was better off without them.

"Why did you come to town, angel?" he asked.

"To show these people how much I love you, that we're a package deal…and to prove to you that your place is here, with me." I lifted his hand and kissed his scarred knuckles. "That not everyone is against us."

"And if your plan didn't work?" His voice was so deep now, I felt it as much as heard it.

I looked up at him, staring into those gorgeous eyes. "Then I planned on selling and going with you. I'd follow you to the other side of the world if I had to."

I could tell he was struggling to find something to say, so I lifted up on my tiptoes, wrapped my arms around his neck, and dragged him down for a kiss. His arms banded around me instantly, lifting me off the pavement as he straightened, and he kissed me back in front of everyone.

When he lifted his head, he murmured against my lips, "I love you, too, Abigail Smith."

• • •

We were close to home, and the cab of the truck was electric. God, I was almost vibrating.

If I had my way, we would have pulled over already and I would have ravished him on the side of the road. But he'd turned me down flat when I'd tried to convince him. He wanted to take his time, he'd said.

I thought I might die if he didn't touch me. Now.

Something splatted against the windshield…

"Is that…?" Another splat, then another followed. "It's rain, Elijah!" I whooped and did a happy dance in my seat. "Finally!"

I was still dancing around excitedly when we reached

home. Eli shoved the door open and was out before the truck finished rocking. He rounded the front, yanked my door open, and lifted me out. I wrapped my arms around him, and he kissed me.

The rain was pouring now, running over the cracked, dry earth, soaking into our clothes. When he lifted his head, I flung mine back and laughed. We were soaked by the time we made a break for the barn.

Hazy light filtered in through the small window, and the rain pounding against the tin roof was the only sound I could hear above our laughter. We reached for each other at the same time, tearing at our clothes, too desperate to even make it up the stairs to Eli's room.

We were both naked, skin slick and slippery in minutes. Eli tugged an old picnic blanket off the rack beside us and threw it on the floor. We went down together in a heap. His large body covered mine, his powerful thighs shoving mine apart, then his heavy cock was there, right where I needed him. He tilted his hips back, taking my mouth as he slid inside me.

His lips never left mine; even when we weren't kissing our mouths were touching.

"Tell me you love me," I rasped.

We were sliding, writhing against each other. "I love you, angel. More than anything or anyone in this world." His grip tightened. "You're mine and I'm yours and nothing…*nothing* will ever change that. You made me whole, sweetheart. You've given me everything."

The beautiful fierceness he communicated in his declaration had me crying out. He pounded into me harder, and all I could do was hold on, chanting that I loved him, too.

Then I was tipping over the edge, still wrapped in his arms.

He stayed planted deep inside me, mouth against mine, swallowing my cries as he fed me his groans, coming hard.

When we both stilled, he rested his forehead against mine. "Thank you, angel, for giving me you."

I wrapped my arms tighter around him, smoothing my hands over his wide back. "You don't need to thank me," I whispered. "I was always meant to be yours."

Then he kissed me and started moving, slow and easy, making love to me again.

Epilogue

Two years later

I stood on the porch, sipping my tea and watching Eli in the field with our new farmhand. He was young, but Eli had recognized the boy's affinity with horses as soon as he saw him with one. He was moving into Eli's old place above the barn on the weekend so Elijah could start training him.

Since Elijah and I had gotten together, a lot of things had changed, so much so that it sometimes boggled my mind. The business had expanded. Now we not only trained horses, but we bred them, too. We'd taken on several new hands, and the place was thriving. In only a short time, we'd almost paid off our mortgage, and I knew without a doubt we'd survive any future curveballs Mother Nature threw at us. And thankfully, for not just us but everyone in this town, we no longer had to worry about Connor Jacobson. The manager of Deep River Bank had recently retired and moved away. I'm pretty sure the move had more to do with Earl Thompson threatening to string him up after catching him cheating with his wife. But whatever the reason, we were happy to see the back of him.

It also hadn't taken long for Cassie and Garrett to come around. Eli had won them over with his quiet strength and unwavering loyalty. They'd seen the way he was with me, the way we felt about each other. It was hard to miss.

And now when we went into town, Eli got the respect he deserved. Yeah, there were still people who were wary of him, refusing to let go of his past, but they were the minority. And those people didn't matter to either of us.

He handed a bucket to the new farmhand and glanced up, catching my eye, and I could see, even from this distance, a smile curl his lips. He smiled a lot now, too. All the time. And every time he aimed that smile at me, I felt it right down to my bones. He said something to the boy beside him, then headed my way, long legs eating up the distance. I couldn't take my eyes off him. He was magnificent in every way.

When he finally hit the steps, I put down my tea and waited for him to reach me. He pulled me into his arms, one of those beautiful work-roughened hands dropping to my belly, cradling my baby bump.

"That was a short nap," he murmured against my hair.

I covered his hand with mine. "This little guy decided to do some line dancing."

"Our boy would never line dance."

We'd found out the baby's sex, and going by the size of me, he took after his father. "Just because you don't like to dance doesn't mean our son won't."

He pulled me closer and swayed from side to side. "Who says I don't like to dance?"

"Getting you to dance at our wedding was like pulling teeth."

"We have our own special dance, angel." There was a little growl to his voice. "When we're alone, and you're naked."

I shivered. "Stop it. You know what I'm like at the

moment." He only had to look at me and I jumped him. All this touching and growling and talking about our "own special dance" was doing things to me.

He cursed under his breath. "Don't tempt me. Not when there's no way I can have you." He tilted his head to the field.

I kissed his throat, and his big body shuddered against me. He growled, and I chuckled softly. "Sorry."

He squeezed my ass. "You will be."

Now I was shivering, too.

He took my hand. "You know how much I hate leaving my wife wanting, but I promise to take real good care of you later."

"Your wife is more than agreeable with that idea," I whispered.

He gave me a squeeze. "Stop teasing and come with me. I want to show you something."

He led me across the yard and into the barn. Both doors were wide open, which meant he hadn't taken me there for privacy...more's the pity. Beside the workbench was something covered in a sheet. "What's that?"

"Your surprise." His cheeks darkened, and he bit his lip.

God, I loved it when he did that. "Well, are you going to show me?"

"If you don't like it, or it's not what you want...I won't be offended, okay?"

He was so serious, nerves started dancing in my belly. "Sure, okay."

He pulled off the sheet and stepped back, crossing his arms and watching me closely. A cry burst past my lips. I stood there rooted to the spot, blinking rapidly.

"Abi?"

"Oh my God," I whispered, tears gathered in my eyes.

"Does that mean you like it?"

I smiled so wide my face ached, then I clapped my hands,

doing a silly little dance. "Do I like it? It's the most exquisite crib I've ever seen. Did you make it?"

"Yes."

I rushed him, and he scooped me up in his arms. "I love it." I peppered his face with kisses. "And I love you."

He wrapped his arms around me tighter, then I carried on covering him in kisses while he threw his head back and laughed.

Acknowledgments

To my amazing family for always being so supportive every step of the way. I love you guys.

My wonderful editor Karen Grove, thank you for your editing genius. I'm so glad you thought of me for this superhot new line. I had such a blast writing this story!

Nicola Davidson and Tracey Alvarez, friends, fellow authors, and overall lifesavers—I'm glad I don't have to do this without you!

To the supportive, encouraging, just plain awesome bloggers, reviewers, and readers I've met along the way—you guys rock!

About the Author

Sherilee Gray writes sexy, edgy, contemporary romance. Stories full of heat and high emotion, following stubborn characters as they fight against the odds...and getting their happily ever after. She's a Kiwi girl who lives in beautiful New Zealand with her husband and their two children. When not writing or fueling her voracious book addiction, she can be found dreaming of far-off places with a mug of tea in one hand and a bar of Cadbury Rocky Road chocolate in the other.

If you love erotica, one-click these hot Scorched releases…

HANDS ON
Part One of the *Hands On* serial by Cathryn Fox

When hot as hell Danielle Lang showed up and asked me to teach her about sex, I thought I was hallucinating. Turns out the beautiful psychologist needed an extra bit of schooling in all things sexual so she could teach a class. I've got a football career to get back to. And she doesn't want to be a part of my world. There's no way we can be together—so I'm going to make sure I enjoy every sexy second…

SHAMELESS
a *Playboys in Love* novel by Gina L. Maxwell

People say I'm shameless. They're right. I like my sex dirty. It takes a hell of a lot to tilt my moral compass, and I always follow when it's pointing at something I want. Especially when it points straight at the one girl in all of Chicago who's not dying for a piece of me. She's all I can think about, and that's a problem, because she wants nothing to do with me. But I've seen her deepest secrets, her darkest fantasies. Now I just need to show her how good it can feel…to be shameless.

DESIRING RED
a *Dark and Dirty* tale by Kristin Miller

Choosing a werewolf mate who'll be with me until I croak? Pardon me while I take some time to think on it. But a steamy encounter before the final ceremony changes everything. Reaper, the Omega's eldest grandson, is fiercely loyal, scorching hot, and built for pleasure. I've only just met him, but I *need* him like no other. By pack law, Reaper can't have me until the Alpha makes his choice…but Reaper's never been one to follow the rules.

Also by Sherilee Gray

CRASHED

REVVED

WRECKED

CPSIA information can be obtained at www.ICGtesting.com
Printed in the USA
LVOW08s0411060916

503361LV00001B/9/P

9 781682 812907